PIECES OF MY HEART

PAUL GROZINGER

Contents

Black Sheep White Rabbit 1

Ben Dover 3

Performing Monkey 4

Turn Blue 5

Woes 6

Broken Mould 7

Sore 8

Lack of Awareness 9

Go Figure 10

Really Mate 11

Chime 13

Starving Artist 14

Doubt 15

Blood Toll 16

Gurt 17

Delirious Neutrality 18

Life Sucks 19

Just Swell 20

Sobering Day 21

Something Else 22

Supernova 23

Soul Food 24

Art in Reality 25

Man in the Mirror 26

Celia 27

Tease my Disease 28

Go Kart 29

Broke for Riches 30

Happy with Lonely 31

Nonsense 32

Ghetto 33

Obscenities 34

Fear of the Known 35

Brilliant Men 36

Recurring Dreams 37

Autumn 38

All Mighty 39

Feeling Heaven as it Rains 40

Competing and Cheating 41

Probably Nah 42

Untouchable Criminals 43

Tailor Made 44

Masochist Affliction 45

Contrast 46

Gifted 47

Holy Hell 48

Fight 49

Selective Ignorance 50

The Game of Life 51

Fete 52

Every day ends in why 53

Emancipation 54

History 55

Outgoing 56

Unfolding 57

Rain and Fires 58

Stunted 59

Consumed 60

Abyss 61

Duet... 62

Mutiny 63

Buggered 64

Prison Mentality 65

Ghost gum 66

Capitalist Woes 67

Done... 68

Happy Anniversary 69

Retain... 70

Spent 71

Depression my Possession...................................... 72

Road Blocks... 74

Stuck 75

Identity 76

Gift and Curse.. 77

Wrong 78

What a Dick 79

Clint 80

Spout of Waste... 82

Haunted 83

Old Soul 84

The Worst Parts of Me 85

Dwelling 86

Glass Ceiling 87

Failed Attempts 88

Army of Darkness 89

Self-Love 90

Cursed 91

Prey 92

Flare in the Skies 93

Eternally 94

Oblivion 95

Green Tomatoes 96

Shits and Giggles 97

Borne of Vibration 98

Would 99

Healthy Wealthy and Wise 100

When 101

Settling 102

Mind Time 103

Faceless 104

Unaddressed 105

As Such 106

Mutual Understanding 107

Art v Science 108

Mental Prison 109

Calling 110

At What Cost 111

Reflectivity 112

Tourniquet 113

Then Some 114

Bad Company 115

The Gift of Life 116

Behind Enemy Lines 117

Poor Boy 118

Guardian Angel 119

Treasure Box 120

Tangled Mess 121

Hard to Breathe 122

Wanker 123

Stunted 124

Tattoos 125

Forsaken 126

Sorrow Borrow 127

Molecular Dance 128

Offerings 129

Alone in Reserve 130

Taking Shots 131

Two Words 132

Charlie Bucket List 133

Basket Case 134

Caged Hearts 135

I said what I said 137

Vacation 138

Chuckles Next Door 139

The Order of Love 140

Eleven 141

Dad 142

Indifference 143

Doubt 144

Starving Artist 145

Monkey Business 146

Willow Dance 147

I Know 148

Final Say 149

Condemnation 150

Exemplary 151

Zen n Now 152

Inherent 153

Anomaly 154

Good in the Hood... 155

Elf 156

Servant 157

Free 158

Recollection 159

Language Universal 160

Pantomime 163

Bend over Backwards 164

Black Sheep White Rabbit

Yesterday's sorrow forges the poets of tomorrow.
Lots of soul, yet not a feeling to borrow.
Articulate and wise, but painfully hollow,
Forged from suffering for reasons I don't know.

We notice the sunshine but feel the rain and snow.
Words reduce us to tears more often than we glow,
We don't want pain and seldom grow,
It's how we were made; it's all we know.

I always considered this part of me foe,
Holding me back from happiness with misery in tow,
Responsible for all the scars I had to sew.
Hating myself on the inside with nowhere to go.

In this river, there isn't much joy that flows.
Happiness resembles filling an ocean with a hose,
For all the heartbreak, pain, and low blows,
It's my thanks for being life's victim, I suppose

It ain't a fashion statement, like trendy clothes,
More like stigmata, where the blood just flows.
People think I'm to blame for the life I chose,
But poetry chose me as any poet knows.

Ascension of comprehension and nobility grows,
From every broken bone and bloody nose,
They're not merely clever phrases and prose.
They're our love for the world written in x's and o's.

The final act before the curtains close,
Torment we endure in silence, echoes
With the minimal love we have left to dispose,
The ones who taught us hate, this debt we owe.

We converted what you gave us to art for show,
Like a beautifully wrapped gift and a pretty bow.
The hate you shared is now love, you know.
The power of a poet is returning love for sorrow.

Ben Dover

It seems we're not playing in the shallow end anymore,

I done my time as an unworthy child, still a bit sore.

I see things for what they are now, from the ceiling to the floor;

I'd never ask you to do a 180 again, you dirty, stinking whore.

She admitted she was backwards, and I still turned it around,

I was lost and confused and gobsmacked at what I had found.

When she was with me, she wasn't running around town,

When her veil dropped, and my heart shattered, it didn't make a sound.

I spent many years healing from the hell she put me through.

As she moved on the next, hungry for something to chew,

Like the most uncanny chicken, out the coup, I flew,

And she still struggles with agony, and the souls she does accrue.

Performing Monkey

Even when I try to go unnoticed, I stand out like a sore thumb.

Life dealt shit cards; I made shit choices, I couldn't be more numb.

I just wanted to be left the fuck alone, even if I had to survive on a crumb.

I couldn't even have poverty, pain, and privacy to myself; I'm such a poor bum.

I'm not looking to chase the things others chase,

I'm still tying my lace. I don't want a place in the race,

I don't want money, power, status or superficial disgrace.

All I ever wanted was to find lasting peace at my place.

I can't be alone, they never let me be,

I retreated to the ghetto to live in scarcity.

Because I'm different, they're obsessed, I don't know if it's them or me.

I feel like a fucking performing monkey, I just want to be free.

Turn Blue

I'm just a guide bringing motherfuckers back to the mothership.

I serenade them while the bloodsuckers, stick a thorn in my other hip.

Can't walk up my stairs without broken glass or seeing another brother trip.

I made it very clear to all of them, I'm one bad son of a bitch.

The mothership is a place we come from and return to,

To coax a motherfucker home, I will not hesitate to burn you.

I'll push anybody to the edge, but I never made anyone turn blue.

I'm a powerful warrior of love and peace; please don't misconstrue.

I light the way like a lantern for the harsh ride home.

I'm not very tall, I often come across like a rash, snide gnome.

I can be as hard as stone, but at home, I'm soft as foam,

My electric meatball is finally functioning better beneath my dome.

Woes

Celia is a girl as beautiful as a rose.

She has flawless skin and a cute little nose.

She has gorgeous dark hair that flows and flows,

I try to convince myself I don't have a crush; my nose just grows.

She has a mind so attractive; she always just knows,

She shows up at the right times, like my friends the crows.

She writes poetry so beautiful, a genius with prose.

She gives me goosebumps with her words, like when the cold wind blows.

I never know what she'll say next; she always keeps me on my toes.

She has something special that keeps me coming to all her shows.
I've known plenty of girls who lack class; I don't want to look at those,

Sometimes, I daydream about the future, that it was my heart she chose.

Broken Mould

My son has a beautiful heart, such a caring, perfect soul.

He's what makes my life worth living, what makes me feel whole.

He taught me so much about love and a loving father's role,

I'm dumbfounded at how my father could steal what he stole.

Stealing from himself, escaping the pain, perhaps his goal.

He shared with me but kept most of what's in the bowl,

It burnt me to the core, still haunted by the scold,

I promised myself I cannot share it, so it's mine alone to hold.

I know it wasn't his, to begin with. Through the generations, it rolled,

Keeping it from continuing in an attempt to be so bold.

It's plagued my existence, my soul I've almost sold.

The love of my son, the cost, if I fail to withhold.

He'll never know what taunts me; by myself, I'm always trolled;

my personal hell, I stay to see his beautiful life unfold.

I guess I was born to break the cycle when they broke the mould.
When my son says, "I love you, Dad," it's all I need to be told.

Sore

I've been through depression, nervous breakdown, psychosis and
more.

Continuously re-open scars when they close just like a door.

Spent far too much time scraping my sorry arse up off the floor.

Tired of this life, my head, heart, and body are constantly sore.

At school, I was great at legal studies. I was going to study law,

I decided I didn't want to spend my life around scum every day
anymore.

I became a carpenter. It was good at first; I didn't think I'd be
poor,

A foolish mistake cost my livelihood, cutting my fingers off with
a saw.

Love has been punishment; I'm amazed I still love that stinking
whore.

I raised my son alone for 14 years, the only human I adore.

Digging my way from the depths of hell, alone I scratch and
claw;

I wonder if life will ever not feel like such a fucking chore.

All the shit I've been through, my wounds still bleeding and raw,

Pain alternates with numb, approaching my final straw.

Still, I try with all that I am, just as I did before,

Maybe tomorrow brings brighter days; who knows what's in
store?

Lack of Awareness

I've been a loser so long I have a real fear of success.

I've become far too comfortable being lazy in my mess.

Taking a leap of faith evokes unimaginable stress;

failure to jump confirms a choice to settle for less.

Focusing on origins left symptoms to impress.

An impression was made with invasiveness.

Now, it's on me to swiftly place this pest

beyond my door as an unwelcome guest.

A comfort zone is a dangerous place, I guess,

A bit sneaky and cunning, somewhat insidious.

It pins me in a way I can't tap the canvas.

Choking me out, I feel dizzy and hopeless.

I feel defeated by nothing, trapped with cowardice.

What the fuck am I afraid of happiness?

I'm finding I sought a lack of awareness;

in hiding, I rort my desire for success.

Go Figure

I'm unlocking all that is deep inside of me,

I don't want to go there, I re-route constantly.

I still hate the concept of home, in perpetual jeopardy;

how do I rest and heal when that place is hell for me?

Home is merely a concept, really.

A projection of feelings about memory.

I had to delve a little deeper before I could see;

I don't hate home so much as what's inside of me.

I was fearful to inhabit my own body.

It became a storage facility, instinctively,

Filled to the brim with my horror, personally;

Ensured home would be hell perpetually.

It was never about location; the place was a trigger,

Luxurious or slumming it, smaller or bigger,

Made little difference; I still felt like a nigger.

It only dispersed when I faced myself; go figure.

Really Mate

All my former friends are too good for me now because their bank accounts have been filled.

Most of them are in real estate; they do very well, selling houses just like the ones I build.

They're in air-conditioned offices and prestigious cars while I slave in the sun, getting grilled.

I cut my fingers off, wrecked my back with heavy lifting, litres of blood I spilled.

I live in a shit hole in the hood, whereas they live high upon a hill;

without builders, they would have nowhere to live and nothing to sell.

But clearly, they're too good for me because they are doing so well.

For someone who works for satisfaction over money, it's a bitter pill.

Social injustice and economic inequity come in many forms.

I can handle being at the bottom of the barrel; I've weathered many storms.

If you are not part of the solution, you are part of the problem, one informs.

Could I sell my soul for riches? I think I'll leave that to the worms.

What I have cannot be bought, nor sold.

One of very few who still has a soul.

My body may be broken and feeling old;

But I'm repairing that, and my soul is still gold.

Chime

I come across as dumber than most people most of the time.

The irony I find frustratingly sublime,

A surreal realization of the blind.

Voiceless yet expressing melancholy, much like a mime.

I come across dumber and dumber, time after time,

As my bells of ignorance continue to chime.

Perhaps I refuse to see what is actually mine,

So I dream and hope, and write another rhyme.

Swinging back and forth the way a pendulum swings,

I still wish I could lose my head in a trade for wings. They call them demons and hell and evil things,

Trying to find lift amongst all the devilish beings.

I don't even know anymore; what am I seeing?

I know it has my heart sick and my soul fleeing,

My prison of flesh, my soul, my being,

Feels immense hopelessness; dogs with cocked legs peeing.

Starving Artist

I'm pretty sure I qualify as a starving artist.
I eat pretty well, but I'm starved of life's goodness.
Compassion, purpose, love, or a woman's touch:
All these things have a price tag attached.

I don't think it is food the artist longs for,
Nor money or applause the singer writes songs for.
It's not notoriety or immortality for the sculptor,
I think they're all love-scorned, mistreated, and sore.

It may very well have been days since I've eaten.
Food seems unimportant when my heart and soul are beaten.
How do I recover what was taken by a cretin,
Without being forced to commit a similar sin?

Describe it in my art's description,
Paint a vivid, detailed depiction,
Rely upon art like my addiction:
A starving artist with the artist affliction.

Doubt

People are so quick to judge and label as if they know who I am.

These little poems offer clues to help them understand,

Self-expression is therapeutic, but on the other hand,

I doubt I'll be understood in conditioned minds so bland.

Those who are better than me and insist on competition

Will never be able to grasp my life's mission.

The human condition, coupled with my personal decision,

I have no desire to get those people to listen.

It may seem paradoxical or hypocritical to many.

Who am I to make a judgment on any?

Even if they seem sociopathic, obsessed with plenty,

If money blows your hair back, I'll bet you a twenty.

My doubt is as valid as your self-appointed superiority.

We exist in two very different worlds, seemingly;

perhaps my need to be understood gives me inferiority.

The larger one's ego, the less room they have for empathy.

Blood Toll

I'm learning to control myself with itches I can't scratch.
I'm on a roll with my health, stitches, and an eye patch.
I didn't get in a fight this time; it's not even like that,
I don't think they made me from the right batch.

The blood tickles and agitates as it rolls down my face
because I overlooked the wound in that place.
The pain comes and goes, but the irritation? It stays.
And this is one of my better ones, not one of my shit days.

In the absence of pain, the itch returns to a gash.
How much more blood must my face splash?
To remember the pain without living it, the task.
How do you get a potato from a bowl of mash?

Every time I forget and behave as though I'm whole,
I'm reminded that a warm, slow tickle must roll.
To forget for a moment is a relieving console;
Until I scratch the itch reminded of the blood toll.

Gurt

Where I come from, you need a strong heart to win. Drugs, crime, and broken souls; gurt by graffiti and sin. No need for a tonic or a glass, just a bottle of gin,

The bottle as empty as this life; still, I can't manage a grin.

These people are products of a sick, deranged system:

A melting pot of misery, and somehow, I fell in with them; for the vast majority, it's a place of no return.

Stuck in the fire for so long, we're addicted to the burn.

People judge, and they're so quick to ridicule,

As if the locals don't already feel minuscule.

Part of the problem is the past and its residual,

Another is systemic illness, which we all contribute to.

When you're driving through the hood being sickened by our shame, Or riding your high horse with your wealth and fame.

The responsibility belongs to whom? Is it indifference to blame? Our past and your present contribute all the same.

Delirious Neutrality

I have the capacity for serious brutality.

I try to remain in a state of delirious neutrality.

Self-control has never been my forte,

Strangling my own choker chain is my sad reality.

It almost seems cruel to have been built this way:

An overload of power with no outlet but disarray.

I have to practice restraint every single day,

To avoid anger and violence and the games they play.

I know what I have in store if I ever need it,

Its dormancy doesn't mean it's gone or retreated.

Fighting it my whole life, and I cannot beat it.

It induces fear rather than pride; I'm far from conceited.

Life Sucks

I'm a mess at best and always settle for less.

With the shit I've been through, I should have an 'S' on my chest.

I'll give some details and spare you the rest,

I want no pity, and you won't be impressed.

Slowly working through the pain I was bestowed,

I see myself as hideous, worse than a toad.

I spent a long time blaming on a lengthy road,

In getting to know myself, the destruction has slowed.

I can't lie; I still have a way to go.

I'm slowly learning what to keep and throw.

Retaining the ills I was sure to know,

destroyed me from the inside blow by blow.

Untangling the chaotic web of destruction,

I'm redefining myself and learning to function.

Like an old vacuum cleaner losing its suction,

I was stuck for so long, married to dysfunction.

Just Swell

As I purge my soul with words,
It's like taking a really satisfying turd.
My burdens disappear in the sky like birds;
It's even more cathartic than I heard.

Poetry and dishonesty don't go hand in hand.
To some, it sounds like fiction; to some, it seems bland.
A broken soul seeking therapy wasn't what I planned,
But here I am, owning my demons with a pencil in hand.

The subject matter is personal and, to me, very real.
Making a spectacle of my shame as the layers I peel,
I say it is the best way I can share the way I feel.
It's the most effective method I've found to help me heal.

I wish I had better stories to tell,
I wish it didn't take forty years to know me so well,
I spent thirty years trapped in my own personal hell.
I wish I could introduce a better man, but oh well.

Sobering Day

The world I live in is very different from yours.

On this basis, I find myself drawn to flaws.

For the same reason I want to escape, you open doors,

I don't know if I'm coming or going, taking a bow or giving applause.

I've spent my life picking myself up from various floors,

Sailing from one bad place to even more precarious shores.

Only once knocked on the heavens, but mostly, the scariest doors.

I fought hard to be here against life's hairiest claws.

They say hell is something you carry with you,

But how did you get it? Did you choose?

If you could choose heaven, then why drugs and booze?

It's a sobering day when the fact of the matter hits you.

Some things can be healed, and some are forever yours.

No two realities are the same in this world of ours.

Be kind to your fellow man; you know not his scars.

If you can't handle your liquor, stay away from bars.

Something Else

In some people, you have to look a bit harder for decency.
It's obvious, but it was brought to my attention just recently,
How easily led the sheep can be.
I don't know why, but it seems everyone wants a piece of me.

Dog-eat-dog made an absolute beast of me.,
An appetite for man's best friend, Korean teppanyaki,
I'm sick of bending over backward to help them see:
What cannibals do when they become hungry.

With an appetite for destruction of each other, we feed:
As though mother nature didn't provide what we need,
it's never enough, lost in our greed.
So we prey on each other as we cry and plead.

To be on top, you must have speed.
And the moral conscience, you can impede.
To call it a dog fight is an insult to their breed,
We are something else, the way we make each other bleed.

Supernova

As I sharpen my pencil, I don't know what I will write next.

It spills out of me effortlessly, as though it is my text.

As I read back over it, my heart and mind checks,

If it is in fact, my soul that I express.

Most of it is trauma-related; I wish it weren't so.

But I've only been where I've been and only know what I know.

Comparison really is a thief of joy; it steals the show.

Like a fish in the Mariana Trench, in the dark and cold, I glow.

My body cramps daily, and my head aches constantly.

I have much bigger problems than what people think of me.

Still, I get stuck on the opinions of many:

A star is dead; there is a black hole void in me.

With countless stars in a single galaxy,

I was born on the day of my star's expiry.

I don't know much about astronomy,

But life seems a dark, cold vortex just for me.

Soul Food

Nearly everything I read has an impact on me.

I want to reach people in the same way through poetry.

Just because it's said rhyming and artistically,

The format does not deduct authenticity.

I've always been an emotional person, intrinsically.

Depth of emotion doesn't remove my word's validity.

I could write more about facts and philosophy,

About butterflies, rainbows, and serendipity.

Fraudulent expression creates an illusion of reality.

Said reality is prone to the laws of individuality,

To paint a false picture would be sad to me,

And to myself, I can't lie, so my poetry is honesty.

There is a certain power in surrender, but not retreat.

To accept what is: food for the starving to eat,

Acceptance and submission are two different treats:

The one you choose determines if the perp or victim eats.

Art in Reality

Art has been my salvation to a degree.

When my head gets too much, art sets me free.

I can't paint on canvas or sing on key,

But I find pursuits to help me forget I'm me.

Mother Nature has always impacted me with her staggering displays.

I'm captivated by beauty and creativity in countless ways.

Art has infinite faces, and no two are the same,

Versatility, diversity, and practical magic incorporated in my days.

Music is like my therapist; it affects me on so many levels.

Literature is like a tour guide taking me on travels.

Cuisine tantalizes the sense as I bask in its revels;

The human body, in all its forms, is art that unravels.

I love gardens, and sculptures, and architectural design.

I love art as obscure as the making of fine wine.

I became an incredible cook, on art, I love to dine;

If I could spend the rest of my days creating art, that would be divine.

Man in the Mirror

I still can't stand my reflection.

Regardless of how thorough the inspection,

I avoid looking in the mirror's direction;

It makes me feel sick, like a disease or infection.

I'd never expect to see perfection,

That would be a ridiculous suggestion.

I still find myself stuck on one question:

Why is it that when I see myself, I feel rejection?

More importantly, what is the solution?

My view of myself is my mind's pollution!

How do I isolate only that section?

And create some form of real interjection?

Celia

I came across a stunning lady on the internet, and she has become my muse.

From the very first poem she read to me, I was overcome by what ensues.

The flood of raw emotion, the depth of soul, how could anyone refuse?

She inspired me so much I decided to write her a poem: what have I gotta lose?

I could only hope to exhibit the talent, beauty, and courage you display.

You wear your heart on your sleeve and put yourself out there day after day.

With the courage to persist in being who you are, despite what the critics say.

The purity of your heart and breathtaking beauty have really helped shift dismay.

I haven't written anything in quite a while because I've been going through a lot.

You inspired me to scribble again, so I thought I'd give it a shot.

I'm so glad I have a muse; I've never seen one so hot,

Stumbling on you was a trip worth taking, but I think I've lost the plot.

Tease my Disease

I no longer live in fractured worlds;

Where everything is separate but somehow compiled.

What was never mine, into the abyss I hurled,

Now, everything is coming together and getting reconciled.

I'm moving into my most powerful state of being,

I'm actively doing something about the hate I'm seeing.

I finally relieved myself, like when you wait for peeing,

I made it to the day of the great agreeing.

I'm not completely at peace as my work doesn't cease; as long as they say please, I cannot be at ease.

I feel like Robin Hood after I fleece the police

I'm invincible, even I can't tease my disease.

Go Kart

You cannot hate a man who has no hate in his heart.

I don't know why you would even want to, for a start.

To hate without provocation, man's made it an art;

To divide and conquer keeps us a little bit apart.

Alone at the window, I stand and stare,

At the disaster unfolding in the sky, no flare

Cast a spotlight on the perpetrator if I dare.

He's standing in the mirror; I'm right there.

Good man's failure to act, as dastardly as evil, doing its part.

I want a better world for our children, but I don't know where to start. My ambition and sense of duty you couldn't plot on a chart,

I've spent my whole life looking for wheels for my kart.

In times of darkness, I undoubtedly return to art.

It made sense that it may be a good place to start.

Stains trickle down my sleeve from my bloody heart;

I need to get this show on the road and find wheels for my kart.

Broke for Riches

This world and I are mutually forsaken.
The struggle isn't obvious; it's beyond blatant.
Man is the enemy, I'm not mistaken,
I refuse to be one of the masses complacent.

All that was right has slowly been taken.
The world has been raped by the rats and their racing.
People don't care just what's at stake and
I refuse to participate in the world's defacing.

Life has destroyed me as man has destroyed the planet,
Destined to be tainted until we can no longer stand it,
No other animal but the ones who ran it,
Can lay claim to a crown of thorns so candid.

It's lonely and dark being one with nature,
Attacked from all angles by the human rapture,
Solely responsible for every little fracture.
Everything you broke for riches will be yours to capture.

Happy with Lonely

The dark night of the soul will end when I lose sight of the goal.

Fixation on destination seems, for me, a great obstacle.

Only when I empty my mind do I truly become whole.

Like the vision impaired seeing clearly through a spectacle.

For so long, I thought the world broke me when it was merely my perception.

The past holds pain, and the future holds hope; both my fixation.

I had depth of soul and purity of love in anticipation.

That's not possible to find, trapped in your own personal rejection.

It's true that the past was the catalyst for the way I hate myself,

Forced to somewhat become a reflection of everybody else.

Like everyone else, I don't love me, but I hate me the best.

I proved I was better, punishing myself until there was nothing left.

They got the ball rolling, so I showed them how to do it properly

As if my annunciation and diction were impeccable, whilst they spoke cockney.

No one could hate me more than me, a fact of certainty,

When I realized what had happened, I became happy with lonely.

Nonsense

I miss my son more than I've ever missed anything;
it's harder to tolerate than an injury or sting.
I feel the best part of me is missing;
without him, my heart doesn't sing.

One of the hardest challenges I've ever had to face:
Me being here and him in another place.
I'm only doing it to repair his mother's disgrace. Before
he was two, she disappeared without a trace.

I raised him solo up until adolescence.
For him, I encouraged her to attempt recompense.
She was never very bright, just a bit dense,
Yet again, her mistakes have me feeling tense.

I never kept him from her; she was responsible for the absence.
She failed him, and now I must suffer; it makes no sense.
It's only a matter of time before she returns to the nonsense.
I really can't stand being on this side of the fence.

Ghetto

Where I live is not a nice place.
Seemingly by choice, a collective disgrace.
The ugliness stains me and wets my face;
Cannibal dogs and broken hearts compete in a race.

You can't blame anyone for how it became this way.
Like an experiment gone wrong, many factors at play.
The lowest of low, it's like society's drip tray;
A place where morality has no place to stay.

Not unlike prison, we keep our backs to the wall.
Primitive people, like babies, who can only crawl.
Surrounded by vultures awaiting your fall,
They don't hate each other; they just don't walk too tall.

They are both perpetrators and victims in a tangled mess,
A reflection of being human in a pool of cess.
Social and cultural conditioning at its best,
It's always the tortured souls that settle for less.

Obscenities

My whole family done turned their backs on me.

I don't blame them; from me, I wanted to be free.

Nobody wants to be around misery,

If they contributed to the cause especially.

I had over one thousand dark nights; depression never had such a grip on me.

I lost my partner, license, job, and house all in one week.

I struggled with addiction, all sad and lonely.

The people I loved most didn't want to know me.

"I wonder if that branch will hold my weight" whenever I pass a tree.

I nearly swerved at oncoming trucks regularly.

The whole experience was far more bitter than sweet.

But at least I know where I stand with my family.

I'm past that now and in recovery,

Tormented by the fact no one can love me.

When I needed love most, there was no one to be seen.

I still don't know if it was me or them who behaved more obscene.

Fear of the Known

I'm in real bad shape; I'm a total mess. It's

not even recovery or ridiculous stress,

It's the joke of my design being put to the test.

I'm terrified of myself; I'm not like the rest.

I feel the raw power, and it's more than I've ever been.

It's so hard to explain things only felt, not seen.

I'm consumed with fear and tired of being in between.

If I go out with a bang, I'm gonna make a scene.

It's crazy serious, and I don't have any plans.

I must channel this power to dance,

In this relationship, I wear the pants.

My hazy, delirious, hypnotic trance.

Brilliant Men

There have been so many brilliant men.

Leo Davinci, Albert Einstein, Stephen Hawking, and Charles Darwin:

They were so vastly different but had some things in common.

Questions around who, why, where, what, and when.

Undying intense curiosity is one element that sets apart them.

To marvel at the miraculous flower, knowing you only hold the stem.

A powerful fascination from physics to bio to chem,

Meticulously artistic in approach, as individual as one's phlegm.

It is only your throat that will coat in the end.

Our bodies reject ill; in futility, we defend

It seems rather seamless; into history, we blend.

To our sons and daughters, what is the message we send?

Perhaps we will design our untimely descent.

Nobody knows for sure the purpose, for we are meant

Que sera to tipi, we all build our tent.

Keeping none safe from the dissident.

Recurring Dreams

At this point, I'm just waiting and hoping to die.

I can try to live convincingly to myself; I cannot lie.

Life has been hell how the fuck did I survive?

It's left my body scarred and took my will to be alive.

Life is hollow in the absence of love, this I can't deny.

I've never been able to love myself; the well was always dry.

Finding love in another only as empty as what was mine,

The older I get, the more sour I become drinking vinegar, I whine.

Fulfillment taunts and mocks me as unattainable in plain sight.

I'm fundamentally broken, comparatively not quite right,

The morning is my nightmare of death; I dream at night.

A battle I cannot win. I've grown weary of the fight.

The only darkness at the end of my tunnel, ironically, is my light.

Blaming others and myself left me bitter and contrite.

Any desires I had fled like a thief in the night.

Swearing like Kurt, "I don't have a gun," on the chrome, I would bite.

Autumn

Like the leaves of a tree, things fall away from me.

Ideas, people, and possessions, many now unseen.

Similar to the life you cling to, we fall eventually.

It shouldn't provoke fear; death is life's only guarantee.

I'm learning to release all things held close to me.

No good comes from fear of reality or clutching vanity.

It was a weakness of my character; it fell from this tree.

Holding things impermanent is why falling is scary.

Empires, beliefs, and systems all fall inevitably.

It's essential for growth, an ever-changing reality.

Autumn has become my favorite season; I can visibly see.

As the leaves fall, so too will we all, not meant to always be.

It's a hard part of life; observing death is not easy.

When loved ones die, we feel we hate the whole tree.

Going with the flow is so difficult, consumed by grief,

Consoled only by the fact spring is autumn's legacy.

All Mighty

I'm training to be god, although I already am.

A contradiction of sorts he who is "I AM."

This very instant, I could die and

It would make no difference to the game plan.

I've overcome the shackles of my meat prison.

Something about my spirit feels like it has risen

Part of the divine plan was my decision.

No preacher, only to myself I listen.

I refer to myself as a god in the most humble manner.

You'd probably call me a tool; I'm a spanner,

I'm a stone, a tree, an insect, the divine planner.

I'm a baby, a child, a father, and a nanna.

He who is I AM is he who YOU ARE.

He is the sun, our life-giving star.

He's in me, and he's in you; he's near and far.

He is the snow that falls and the airbag in your car.

He's everything and nothing in perfect synchronicity.

He's in all of life, the all-encompassing duplicity.

I have not finally succumbed to my former insanity,

I just know that I am a god without vanity.

Feeling Heaven as it Rains

The stillness and silence are me.
The motion and noise are my brain.
It's difficult to digest and harder to see;
with no conflict, neither is slain.

The perfect partnership, most definitely.
Cohesion means no imbalance remains.
Compulsive thinking is the enemy.
To this, the imbalance pertains.

My mind always takes over; I just want to be.
My head has become shackles and chains.
To realize this prompted my recovery,
To feel heaven as it rains.

I've always been curious about synchronicity;
What it has to do with personal gains.
I've applied it with great simplicity.
To match the frequency of me and my brain.

Not like anything I could describe effectively.
Trying to convey it, my mind strains.
Applying synchronicity to my mind and me,
Has alleviated so many pains.

Competing and Cheating

In the modern world we live in, my hopes and dreams are fleeting.

Life's like a broken record on the worst verse repeating.

People in my audience laugh and mock even before finding their seating.

My desire to offer the gifts I have is slowly dying and depleting.

People are somewhat a reflection of me; it's only themselves they're mistreating.

Like cutting flesh from your own bones, in need of good eating,

there will be no winners when it's only ourselves we are beating.

Like sitting for a test knowing the only way to pass is cheating.

It probably sounds like I'm just moaning and bleating,

Expressing my discontent for sure; life systematically defeating.

A unified higher order of existence seems a mere pipe dream.

With capitalism, religion, and immorality, the only way to live is competing.

A shake of the hand for the knife in your sleeve is our standard way of greeting.

I don't want to be met with contempt; I want more soul upon meeting.

The fragility of the human condition, to our controllers, is a very neat thing

I endeavor to unveil our collective foolishness as long as my heart is still beating.

Probably Nah

Balance is a bitch, especially when the scales have been tipped for so long.

I'll upset a lot of people with honesty, and many will say I'm wrong.

Slurp those muddy waters and have another toke on the bong.

Maybe my honesty will help me find a place where I belong.

I believed I was inferior and was treated as such all along.

With an upgraded perspective, I will no longer sing that song.

It might be provocative to those who done me wrong,

It's been coming since forever; they made me too strong.

I didn't choose for this trauma to retain,

I did choose to get things right in my brain.

I won't bore you with details of what I overcame;

The most confronting thing I've had to do was to refrain.

Now, I see things for what they are.

I consciously choose not to return a scar,

You will know if it's about you, near or far.

Would an apology make a difference? Probably nah.

Untouchable Criminals

Medical professionals have made me ill.

Lacking competence and regulation is a licence to kill.

I've always feared general practitioners and do still,

In an industry where fatal incompetence should be nil.

I've only trusted one doctor in my life. Paid a

visit when my health was in strife,

Went back for the same thing at least ten times.

Rather than doing his job, he stuck in the knife.

It's all in your head, he kept assuring me.

Obvious pain and symptoms overlooked ignorantly.

Perhaps his diagnosis actually affected me.

His refusal to do his job tipped me over mentally.

False diagnoses prescribing pills not meant for me

Put more than a dent in my identity.

They made me sick and nearly killed me.

Those untouchable criminals made me crazy.

Tailor Made

Could the rise in mental illness be due to tainted evolution?

Perhaps it picked up pace with the industrial revolution.

When money afforded the right to force upon the world pollution,

I don't think a technological revolution was the appropriate solution.

More entitled than ever bound in sensory distraction.

Everything comes at the touch of a button, instant gratification.

"Keeping up with the Joneses," our futile competition,

As we perpetuate in vague awareness our own destruction.

Two-thirds of children in classrooms now on medication.

Spending their time on phones, tablets, and play-station;

A systematic, societal mental eradication,

Individuals, governments, gangs, and corporation.

They point their fingers at each other in this nation.

As people become more ill, I watch in frustration.

Money talks and bullshit walks, political persuasion.

They've force-fed us specific medication for generations.

Masochist Affliction

I made far too many cheap mistakes.

The price was way too much, and still, I paid.

I know accountability is what it takes

The bill was fixed up, and my sanity frayed

I beat myself down time and time again.

I have an appetite for destruction and a taste for pain.

Very few can deliver the hit I crave,

I can hurt myself as easily as stabbing a vein.

I don't condone drug use and have never used a sharp.

When I spill my own blood, I suggest an umbrella or a tarp.

A predisposition given to me right from the start,

A pesky characteristic like an introduced carp.

I hate that I rely on pain so much.

My courage is a real illness, not Dutch.

In the absence of fear, the pain was my crutch.

Others failed to deliver, but I always had the touch.

I'm seriously trying to heal and overcome my affliction.

I get oddly excited whenever I sense friction.

Like a junkie sweating in the devil's kitchen.

I work so hard to maintain control and impose restriction.

Contrast

I respect you all in varying degrees for various reasons.

A forest full of odd trees, even in the scariest seasons.

Some fuel the contempt, happy in their treason,

Some are pretty and poisonous yet promise to be pleasing.

I try to be kind to all of the creatures,

Even those with less-than-desirable features.

Cruelty, greed, and destruction inevitably teaches.

We need love, honor, and creation as land needs beaches.

For if not for the benefit of such contrast,

Could we have a perception so deep and vast?

One extreme ceases to exist without its counterpart,

Just as the gift of the present relies on the past.

Gifted

Happiness is an illusion, peace a mirage,
Suicidal fantasies dangle in the garage.
I do my best to handle the barrage.
My blood is tainted; an illness collage.

It's what I am; I just have to deal with it.
I never cut myself, or I'd peel that shit,
Like morphine nausea, a real sick hit.
I'm not dramatic or narcissistic, that ain't it.

From the day I was born, I was never quite right.
Disgusted by me, I loathe the sight.
Folks are quick to judge, not knowing my plight.
I'd much rather die; still, for my life, I fight.

Every day, I don't kill myself; it's another battle won.
There's no pride in that I've become hollow and numb.
Darkness, my old friend, you are fucking scum.
Depression floods my cells worse than rage from rum.

Holy Hell

Though I don't desire, I keep on trying.

I know I ain't the shit; the flies keep dying.

Hard to live in a mind so violent,

So rarely quiet, but it echoes the silent.

My lord just won't let it end.

So rigid I crack rather than bend,

Promised a life of pain until the end.

My dying wish is to make me my friend.

So fixated on death, I've never really lived.

I hate myself utterly and simply can't forgive.

Strangely, I feel I have something epic to give.

Holier than Thou, I'm a fucking sieve.

Fight

I'm trying to recover from what the world has done to me.

Maybe I did it to myself, but I'm still in recovery.

I didn't know what I was doing; I was taught by nobody.

Who allows these sick animals to run free?

Is it your god, the one they call all mighty?

So imagination is to blame; well, alrighty.

I've battled my mind in sheer futility,

And blamed an entity that no one can see.

It is not god but man who is guilty.

I point the finger at everyone individually.

Every one of you is sick; it ain't just me.

The best aren't exempt, frustratingly.

Fuck I'm going to miss my pain; it's the only one that held me tight.

Dreaming of a white Christmas in the head, I'm not quite right.

I just want to be numb, but there is no cocaine in sight.

So, myself and the world I continue to hopelessly fight.

Selective Ignorance

They say ignorance is bliss, but I think that's incomplete.

Perhaps the word selective should precede,

Total ignorance would be a shallow life indeed.

To turn it on and off like a switch is the feat.

The mind is dangerous when left to roam free.

Complete ignorance is choosing stupidity.

I think bliss resides somewhere in between

Understanding the mind and its complexity.

When I become my own worst enemy,

I've gone to war with a mind-made entity.

Who wins that battle, me or me?

My mind created this duality.

In selecting ignorance, that battle will cease to be.

It was borne out of ignorance, the sweet irony.

To know what to be ignorant of is the key,

To find bliss in the midst of productivity.

The Game of Life

Love, joy, and peace seem so few and far between,

Starved of all that's good in life, craving like a fiend.

Despair, sorrow, and hurt seem the common theme.

Life gave me darkness; towards the dark, I leaned.

The time I borrowed, I wish, was never lent.

My life is a backyard abortion, a coat hanger in a tent.

When you know not of happiness, it devalues your resent.

I either fight out of spite or become content with my lament.

Love is not pain; it's the opposite, in fact.

I can't remember a day my heart was still intact.

When pain invades the heart, one is bound to react.

Of all the gifts I was given, still haunted by what I lacked.

Life gave me so many lemons I'm obsessed with an apple.

A retarded contortionist in a fight club with myself, I grapple.

Dreams of death, lousy choices, and a tendency to babble.

I can't make good words with my letters; this isn't Scrabble.

Fete

Life is a carnival; nobody said it was fair.

So much to do and see, no time to spare.

I've been here so long I'm painfully aware.

I've spent the whole time on the carousel of tears and despair.

Up and down, round and round, through blurry eyes, I glare

At everyone enjoying attractions as I just sit there.

Most of it is a freak show; normality is so rare.

I talk to myself like a nut job, trying not to swear.

I should get off this pony and try another ride if I dare.

I wish I was compelled to try, but I'm not quite there.

So effortless for others in the fun and games they share,

I can't muster the effort to *even* pretend I care.

Sideshows, freak shows, rides, and candy everywhere.

Wanting to participate like jamming a circle in a square,

I wasn't made for this, alone I sit and stare,

I should paint a smiley face to compliment the red nose that I wear.

Every day ends in why

Whenever I wake, the day begins with Why?
I never have the answer when I sleep at night.
In constant wonder on the Sabbath, I cry.
Another week has passed, and still, I sigh.

Life too often feels like a waste of time.
Maybe not for others, but I waste mine.
A forty-five in the right, in the left, a nine.
If guns solved problems, I'd be fine.

Banging caps aimlessly at the sky,
If he were up there, I'd hit Jesus Christ.
Don't get me wrong, I'm very nice.
I patiently await my day to die.

I don't know how, when, where, and why,
But I know someday I'll get my chance to fly.
This life will likely end in classic style,
On a day starting and ending with Why?

Emancipation

Emotional baggage and residual pain have largely dictated my course.

It's no easy task with no apology; they clearly have no remorse.

I was only able to get past this by returning to the source. The source of my true being has offered me recourse.

The damage of the past was not mine to keep.

Only through my mind can it inward seep,

Shutting down my brain was my quantum leap.

I've laid it to rest now, my soul I reap.

I didn't comprehend I had a choice in the matter.

When I made that choice, my pain did scatter.

I know which I prefer between the former and the latter.

It's a mere recollection, all that blood spatter.

I shut down my mind to journey deep inside,

Absolutely terrified of what I knew I'd find.

To accept such atrocious behavior, I couldn't abide.

However, acceptance was the only way to ease my mind.

History

I can feel the life gradually surging back into me.

It's been an arduous road from where I have been.

The depths of despair I refer to as the basement of hell.

Left me a treacherous climb long after I fell.

Heartbreak and addiction are a dangerous combination.

A structure built for the collapse was my life's foundation.

Always a struggle to follow my love of creation,

It's exhausting fighting for my life for mere preservation.

Suicidal fantasies still linger, and my demons still taunt me.

I cannot point the finger when it's what's inside that haunts me.

Peace and purpose are my life's elusive mystery.

As much as death seduces me, perhaps I'm here to make history.

Outgoing

I'm going out because I want to be outgoing.

The grip of depression loosening, my lethargy slowing.

I want more from life, afraid of not knowing,

Throwing caution to the wind while it's still blowing.

If not now, will it ever happen?

I'm at the end of my rope and snappin.

Umbrella drinks and pools I could be lappin.

I just need to use action and quit the rappin.

I've spoken enough; it must be time to turn out

Rollin with the punches hits, I'll churn out.

Somethings I still need to learn bout.

Fast cars and slow women, not the reverse burnout.

Unfolding

It's been a terribly long time since I've seen such positive developments.

I developed into a wreck so easily; it's nice to sense some balance.

I feel good about me and my prospect for another chance.

I've laid to rest so many of my personal torments.

I have more energy, direction, and vivid clarity.

I'm not so fearful of my pit of disparity.

The tail end of that, I'm not sad to see,

Imagine being sad departing with sadness, the sick irony.

Replacing my destructive habits was no easy task.

Underlying causes almost untouchable as they bask.

It required brutal honesty and the removal of my mask.

Now, life's unfolding as it should, what more could I ask?

Rain and Fires

I'm very fond of the smells of fresh rain and wood fire.

The sound on a tin roof sings softly like a choir.

I've found there isn't much left that I desire.

A mountain top where it rains a lot is where I will retire.

I don't ask for much; I have simple desires.

A cabin on a mountain with rain and fires,

In the absence of predators, thieves, and liars.

Maybe even a tree swing made from tires.

To distance myself from "civilization" is my dying goal.

I won't need a woman because I'm already whole.

I'll be more than happy to play that lonesome role.

Perhaps before my heart stops, I can heal my soul.

The nature of man has clearly taken its toll.

I may not even need to dig a hole.

The wildlife is welcome to the flesh on my bones.

Rain, fire, skeleton, trees, and stones.

Stunted

There is something queer
About the people here.
Watching intently _perhaps out of fear.
They need to know but have no idea.

It's curious, to say the least,
Why would anyone choose bones to feast?
A bit fucked up, like a child and a priest.
Where do they go when the laughter has ceased?

Maybe it's the tears of a clown or the agony of a beast,
Pitiful either way, attacking others in search of peace.
Sadness comes in many forms; happiness doesn't tease.
So disturbed by themselves they need another for release.

I wouldn't wish it on anyone, not even my enemies.
A painful way to live, dying on your knees.
If I were offended, I'd be fooled by their desperate, hidden pleas.
Misery cloaked in cruelty these eyes can spot with ease.

Are they a bit slow or just easy to deceive?
Why do they persist when their pain they can't relieve?
Grown-ups that couldn't grow up are still so hard to believe,
Desperately clinging to their method, no hope of reprieve.

Consumed

Admitting that I have fear is something I find difficult.

Ironically paradoxical that I fear acknowledging that I'm afraid,

A manifestation of all I've seen, heard, thought, and felt.

My fear is in the dark, and that has me terrified.

I'm not afraid of the dark but in the dark of what I'm afraid of.

A stranger to fear for so long you would think that he got laid off.

I find myself in a wanting, confusing place of trade-off;

A stranger in a strange place, I don't know what I'm afraid of.

When I finally surrendered to the dark, I fear

Insanity moved me over to take the wheel and steer.

Surreal and profound with a mixture of excitement and fear,

I only vaguely recall why that abyss I fear to go near.

Abyss

I came to the end of my rope and finally lost it.

They locked me up in an asylum, paranoid and psychotic.

Like I reached in my skull, plucked out my brain, and tossed it.

Years of depression and a nervous breakdown, I was neurotic.

I spent five days in the abyss of insanity,

Held against my will, all I had was uncertainty.

I'd gone too far this time, though I was always crazy.

My recollection is twisted, distorted, and hazy.

I was flooded with fear for what had become me.

I didn't think they would ever set me free.

I always knew I severely contrasted mentally,

I didn't think I could escape the prison inside me.

I was vaguely fearful of never returning to reality.

Doctors forced drugs on me for breakfast and tea,

I don't really remember a visit from Aunt Louie.

I was terrified this would be my state permanently.

Surrounded by ill people in captivity,

Not the most conducive for recovery.

On the sixth day, I returned to sanity.

On the seventh day, I convinced them of my normality.

Duet

My desires have been distorted for far too long.

My fires have been thwarted like a cone to a bong.

Comfortably numb trying to find my song,

I hum a tune, rewinding where I went wrong.

Knowing myself is both the problem and the solution.

In hiding from me, I created my own inner pollution,

A very real outcome of self-induced illusion.

I brutalized myself with honesty to get to the truth then.

What I had always desired was merely escape in various forms,

Perhaps due to many memories of precarious storms.

As I gaze into the mirror, the scariest warns,

You don't know yourself shrouded in hilarious norms.

I had to peel back layers and do some sorting.

My whole life felt fake and needed aborting.

I wanted to be higher than the coke I was snorting, So I listened to my heart and soul, the duet they sing.

Mutiny

All I've ever known is internal mutiny.

I found a way inside; I'm shooting me.

The war rages on ruthlessly,

Fighting myself under my own scrutiny.

Upon visual inspection, I doubt you could see

The depth of pain from my adversary.

We are one and the same: he is me.

I never wanted to be an enemy.

Very few have tasted my cruelty.

It cost so much I don't give it freely.

My positive intentions have made me greedy;

what could be your hell is my mutiny.

Studying myself, it seems unnecessary.

Like a timid child, I find it scary.

The way I direct it is my responsibility.

My battle within saves you from me.

Buggered

I'm trying to surrender to the sleep I must receive.

I try to convince myself, though I'm hard to believe.

Why is good rest so difficult to achieve?

My exhausted, weary body I must relieve.

It's not insomnia, but some mental aversion.

Thinking about it only makes it worsen.

Clearing my mind of all its perversion,

I sleep so infrequently it feels like an excursion.

I brought it upon myself to a large extent,

Inability to let go keeps the demons pent.

Why would I choose to hold excrement?

When I'm so fucking tired, I'm really spent.

I'm tired through the day and buggered at night.

Still, something inside me puts up a fight.

Like a swarm of locusts inside taking flight,

Something so fucking simple, and I can't get it right.

Prison Mentality

Since I was very young, anger has been my automatic default setting.

I was mistreated as a child. I couldn't choose what I was getting.

I became spiteful and angry rather than scared and bed-wetting.

I would always swing back over, being fearful or fretting.

I can only behave according to what I know.

I learned early to duck and return the blow.

Running or surrender, was an absolute no-go.

My life became so-so, and my growth was in slow-mo.

I spent thirty years angry and confused, stuck in a loop.

Fighting an intense war as a solitary troop.

I wasn't trying to be tough; it came naturally like poop.

Fed up to the brim, I finally found the scoop.

My anger and spite were hurt in disguise.

I couldn't make it right; I kept hurting guys.

I was brutal with my honesty and cried and cried.

Thirty years in a prison of anger, I was forced to hide.

Ghost gum

I have a ghost gum that has become a friend.

When I say have, I don't mean like a possession.

I forget about everything, even the end.

That's saying a lot about a lifelong obsession.

I feel ill inside at the hands of mankind,

A pale reflection of something dead inside.

If you look too closely, I'm sure you'll find;

Greed, corruption, pollution, and genocide.

The more absorbent you are, the more you tend to hide

From the man in the mirror and the horror inside.

Too often, living life in rewind,

Too often causing strife with my mind.

I let it go with a wave I send.

It seems I finally learned my lesson.

Incessant thought and miserable reflection are a volatile trend

so I lose my mind for moments staring at the ghost gum.

Capitalist Woes

I need to generate some cash flow.

Love don't pay my bills, no.

I despise the rat race, yet I hunger for dough.

Gold may shine, but I'm sickened by the glow.

A harvest we'll reap for the seeds we sew.

Life has a string attached, the capitalist yo-yo.

What gold fever does to people is worse than so-so.

Mediocre would be a compliment; that illness is a no-go.

You can't lead by example, so take note.

Living in poverty ties your hands with the same rope.

I know I must, but in the meantime, I'll hope.

I'd just rather not participate in this sick joke.

Life is largely dictated by the bank note.

Merely a facade, like a coward in a trench coat.

Shooting up the school, pupils have nowhere to go,

Surely, I'm not the only one who thinks we can do better, though.

Done

I made my choices and accept the onus for what's to come.

Handed the baton low in a relay I didn't want to run.

I severely mistreated myself; I was taught by scum.

So many contributing factors will see me done.

Bad habits, my response to a desire to die.

Smoking dope at thirteen and tobacco at nine.

I never felt so low as when I was trying to get high;

expensive regret coughing up my life savings to buy.

I hated myself, never really lived. I merely existed,

Trapped in a cycle of illness and shame, a total misfit,

Born sick and different, my view of life twisted,

Bringing death too soon for more reasons than listed.

Gripped tight by habits of shame and a life never right.

I don't want to be remembered for the smoke that dimmed my light.

I must leave it all behind, the hardest battle I'll fight.

I'll never get it right, but I'm done chasing death out of spite.

The laws of attraction have become a fixation.

Always overlooked obvious ways to change the situation.

I constantly ignored myself, causing the negative reaction.

Then, I blame others and circumstances for my lacking satisfaction.

Happy Anniversary

It was our anniversary yesterday, and I enjoyed it thoroughly.

I didn't feel the need to get drunk; it didn't bother me.

I was always a sucker emotionally and sentimentally.

It's so easy to see we were meant to be... temporary.

As the songs we used to get drunk to played merrily,

It made more sense why we both drank so heavily.

In a partnership of loneliness ceremoniously.

It made me content. I'm now alone, you see.

You dragged me to the pits of hell deceivingly.

I would have followed you anywhere desperately

Alone I sing our songs, still off-key,

Reminding myself that everything is temporary.

What we had was exciting and fun, disastrous and scary.

I should have known from day one as you beckoned the wary.

It's such a relief to not care, finally.

Like all my Christmas came at once, happy anniversary.

Retain

It seems along with fortitude comes a broader range of pain.

The heavier the cloud, the more rain it contains.

The later you are running, the faster the train.

No relief in sight for the one that never complains.

Just because I can handle it doesn't mean I deserve it.

If I saw the hazard, it's hard to say I'd swerve it.

Lacking fortitude would make me more of a victim.

When shit gets real, a boy in a bubble can't curve it.

I don't know if I'm being rational or completely insane.

I look to the sky; before I see stars, I see planes.

It's a part of me I'm actively trying to retrain.

I've been through some shit, but I choose what remains.

Spent

I've spent my life gaining skills and scars.

Many spent theirs gaining cash and cars.

Their lives seem fun and bright.

In the dark, I remain out of sight.

We all have problems; the grass is greener on the other side.

Such is the human condition, creators of genocide.

I may be poor, but I sleep quite well at night.

I have what I need, and my soul is alright.

It's hard enough with the internals wars I fight.

To sell my soul for wealth could never feel right.

My pockets may be empty, but my soul is light.

In a humble way, not to come across contrite.

Depression my Possession

No stranger to depression; it's always been an element of my experience of existence.

I try to allow it to pass quickly by way of permission rather than rejection and resistance.

I've found the more I evade the hell it brings, the more I facilitate its persistence.

A painful lesson to accommodate my brokenness allows it to be temporary past tense.

Today, I was overcome again, flooded by inconsolable, debilitating sadness and agony.

On the precipice of a breakthrough, the overwhelming shadows took hold of me.

Unable to function, ashamed to be seen for the weakness, is my enemy.

The tears uncontrollable, the dark thoughts, comparison, and suicidal fantasy.

I know I must own it and surrender it's never been something I could avoid.

It consumes me so severely it overshadows feeling angry or annoyed.

In vain, I try to mask, divert, or postpone with futile efforts I've employed.

I've tried so many tactics to no avail, makes me want to replicate Freud.

I've resigned to acceptance; I simply must let it do its thing.

To let the pain invade, the tears roll, and the horror it must bring.

To fight it does not help; it elongates that familiar sting.

I will not give into it's will lest it kill the song I sing.

Road Blocks

I feel enlightened, but I'm still chipping away at the chip on my shoulder.

My whole life was like that Greek fellow, going up hill with a boulder.

The pain still cradles me at night; it's my only holder.

I've come so far in such a short time, but I don't feel any older.

I found peace and ascended in some way, shape, or form.

I still struggle to drag myself from what was my norm.

I found my niche, the calm within the storm,

I'm trying to find happiness sitting alone in my dorm.

It's how a contradiction feels or, ironically, living a paradox.

Knowing they're not close to matching and calling them a pair of socks.

My past, present, and future completely unlocks.

For only moments at a time with no road blocks.

Stuck

I've been wrestling with my mind, and it's ever so strong.

I allowed it to remain in control for far too long.

I feel incredibly foolish for being so wrong.

My brain was the cause of separation all along.

It's what separates us from all the other animals in the kingdom.

I've lost my shit plenty but been out of my mind, seldom.

We've claimed the throne, yet we kill everything; well done.

It all originates in the mind; that is the place hell's from.

We project our minds to create insanity and madness.

We protect our minds to maintain grip on disparity and sadness,

like a mother bird sitting on broken shells in the bird's nest.

I still believe Nietsche said many words best.

"God is dead" was famously and controversially said.

I believe it's because God cannot reside in your head.

A concept created there, however, almost never understood.

God can't be experienced if I am stuck in my head for good.

Identity

I always thought I needed an identity,
Someone I could be sure of and claim to be.
I clung to fleeting parts of life desperately.
It took ages to work out what that meant for me.

For so many years, I was blind to see
That too often, I held a memory
Just because I wear the scars to see,
Does not mean that that is me.

All my dreams, the things I'd like to be,
All my past, the things done to me
The car I drive, the clothes I wear, life's superficiality
None of that shit comes close to describing me.

When I worked out what identity meant to me,
I felt ashamed and foolish, essentially.
Residual damage is not actually an entity
Why do I have one anyway? It should be dead to me.

Gift and Curse

I raised my son alone because his mother didn't want to be a part of it.

If I'd known who she really was, I never would have started shit.

That two-faced Gemini did a complete backflip.

It fucked me up pretty bad, but it was my son's heart it hit.

As soon as she was pregnant, she became a completely different person.

Certainly not for the better; that cunt did worsen.

She'd gained control; she had my balls in her purse, then

She made my life hell until she made that curse end.

She abandoned her child before his second birthday.

Doing him a favor instead of raising him the worst way.

She left him in my capable hands so she could party,

I was glad to be rid of her, no need to watch where your birds lay.

Wrong

I've always hated myself because I don't belong;
an accident at birth, a mistake that's wrong.
An outsider to the core, for acceptance, I'd long
Begrudgingly marching to a vastly different song.

If I could be like them, I'd change in an instant.
I couldn't be someone else. I'd always be distant,
Angry at myself, and misunderstood like an infant.
I just wanted to fit in; I rejected me for being different.

I rejected the concept of god and blamed my maker.
I suppressed who I really was and became a faker.
13 to a dozen, but only for the lucky baker,
Wanting the next chance encounter to be the undertaker.

I couldn't possibly love me, it was plain to see.
Feeling more like an alien than a slim minority.
It never occurred to me this might be evolutionary;
perhaps I'm just a highly evolved rarity.

What a Dick

I find it so easy now to marvel at the magic of creation.
I see things more clearly now; not a tragic situation.
I am actually able to be flooded with elation.
I dumped my shit with no more constipation.

Like seeing the world for the first time,
It was not the world, but my eyes covered in grime.
The deluge of majestic beauty looks mighty fine.
To have passed before seeing it would have been a crime.

Even something as simple as a golden sunset,
Contemplating desirable experiences I haven't done yet.
These days, it takes a great deal to get me upset.
Amazing how trauma can make you misinterpret.

I'm still in shock that I could nearly have missed this;
flooded with oxytocin like the sweetest kiss.
I'm slowly learning what gratitude is,
And not just for my large penis.

Clint

Old Smithie got me rotten drunk when I was twelve years old.

Fishing by the river, the night was dark and cold.

First time I'd been really pissed, I was young and bold.

Then my dad says to me, "What would your grandfather think?"
God rest his soul.

I burst into tears instantly. I was a mess.

He died two years prior from a blood clot in the chest.

My dad watched me get drunk, then put me to the test.

Smithies boys gave me shit, laughter, and verbal cess.

Smithie got me wasted, dad tore my heart out, and Clint,
humiliated.

I tried not to show it, but I was fucking devastated.

Then they put me on the waterbed, waited, and anticipated.

I vomited my arse off and woke hungover and deflated.

Six years later, they invited me on a hunting adventure.

I'd just started work and declined for that venture.

Clint got his head blown off in the middle of nowhere.

Luck was on my side; the fact I didn't go there.

At his funeral, I cried like the night at the river.

I don't think he was quite sixteen; the thought still makes me quiver.

I hoped he was laughing at me from wherever.

Smithie said it should have been me who got shot; he wasn't too clever.

It's weighed heavy on my mind for quite some time.

A dark cloud, at times, covers my sunshine.

The death of a child lingers; it's hard to define.

Something about it still haunts me, that child-on-child crime.

It was said to be an accident, but only one man knows for certain.

The fifteen-year-old with the rifle who closed Clinton's curtain.

I forgave him for giving me shit and cackling while I was hurtin'.

He was a wild child; with death, he was always flirtin'.

Spout of Waste

We are in the same, yet a very different place,

Much to mine and your distaste.

Anything but pleasant, a living disgrace.

When decisions are made without due care in haste.

It seems so plainly obvious, staring me in the face.

Choices of others lead to choices of our own misplaced.

The days melt into one another and disappear without a trace.

Like a pouring jug of poison, a spout of waste

Indiscriminate of culture, creed, or race;

A position in which anyone can be placed.

The mighty knows not when he will fall from grace.

The meek knows not if he will find the life he's chased.

Haunted

My father killed a man and so gave me his name.

I guess he couldn't live with his guilt and shame.

A despicable excuse for a man, Billy the lame.

Such a disgrace I refused to use that surname.

Named me after a dead man and then ran from his ghost.

Not before roughing me up, a tough man to boast.

To see the back of him; slow burned like a roast.

To escape his grip and reject his name, I'd like to make a toast.

To William Walker Prescott, your middle name says it all.

Charlie must have known you would run and fall.

Walk slowly in the other direction, but do not stall.

I will show you how death feels. My name is Paul.

Old Soul

I've always felt like what they call an old soul,
As though this existence is not my only role.
Drawing my essence from a collection of all.
Past lives and or parallel dimensions mashed in a bowl.

Perhaps my soul is old for failure to realize the goal,
Similar to a character in a video game console.
Life after life, endless opportunity to continually fall,
Desperately seeking to be a part of something whole.

I don't know for certain, but I sense a heavy toll.
Perhaps in past lives, I murdered, raped, and stole.
My life feels like punishment with my back to the wall.
I'm bursting with accumulation, my spirit is swoll.

How do I not get recycled and cease that role?
Is it based on morality or just protocol?
In this life, I constantly stall.
I don't want to come back; I want to go home.

The Worst Parts of Me

All the worst parts of me didn't flee suddenly.

They departed as though they were free and orderly.

It started without recognition subconsciously.

It accelerated when my dark side met luminosity.

I had this problem where I was afraid of me;

Terrified of what I was potentially.

It was never any secret I came from a bad seed, Taught to taunt myself with the imaginary.

I began to hide from my imagination, naturally.

Holding onto an image of myself involuntarily.

An image I adopted that was never really me;

I introduced my dark to the light, and it was clear to see.

The worst parts of me were always free.

In fact, they never did actually belong to me.

Haunted is not who I have chosen to be.

One by one, with no fuss, my ghosts retreat.

Dwelling

I need a new place to dwell.
I want out of this living hell.
Drugs and dog shit are all I can smell.
What can I say about the neighbors? But oh well.

I made my mistakes, and I've done my time.
Maybe I can escape without being stained by grime,
A land of exploitation, run by crime.
I keep in my garage a shovel and lime.

I've been here long enough to know how it goes,
Wrong place, wrong time, and your blood flows.
I piss a lot of people off, but they're not my foes.
I'll still give them the kiss of death as I hand them a rose.

They avoid me like the plague, and I like it that way.
I keep everything vague and be careful what I say,
Not from fear nor respect; I just do it my way.
I want so badly to get out of here; I await the day.

Glass Ceiling

I've done so much damage now nothing will suffice but healing.

It's taken more than one could imagine to reveal the layers I'm peeling.

Hiding in every dark corner possible rendered me inconsolable and reeling.

I refused to acknowledge in my cowardice exactly what I've been stealing.

My perpetual hell has always had a self-imposed glass ceiling.

Ironically, avoiding pain before the devil, I've been kneeling.

Unable to see the forest for the trees, afraid to feel a feeling,

Ignorant to the depth of emotional hurt, my only way of dealing.

The physical pain has now surpassed the hurt I could never face.

Sickened to the core, left with agony and distaste.

Memories haunt my being as I rewind and retrace

I've beaten myself to come last in a single-man race.

Crippled by incapacity, the sole cause of my disgrace.

Blinded to my weakness, as though I sprayed my eyes with mace.

The horrid creature in the mirror I could never replace.

 Will find solace and redemption emerging from my hiding place.

Failed Attempts

I was born to live this way;

With the rats and the roaches in dismay,

Black and white fade into grey.

I'm a fucking loser, but I ain't scared to play.

Behead it, bleed it, gut it, fish fillet.

I wanted casserole but got mornay.

I could totally hit some quiche, Loraine.

In the devil's kitchen, I sweat in vain.

I see the dark clouds as I await the rain.

I was there for the onslaught stained with pain.

Red, orange, yellow; wash it again.

I hate this life at my hands, I can't be slain.

Army of Darkness

Ravens and bats, I seem to attract.

Always looming overhead, I no longer react.

Maybe it's something about the color black?

Perhaps they, too, have been attacked.

It no longer seems strange; they approach with tact,

Almost as if they had made a pact.

They're not chasing anything they may have lacked;

like an army of darkness above me, I'm backed.

At night, the bat through the day, the crow for many years, I've tracked.

They seem to have no fear of me and relish close contact.

The truest friends I have, to be exact.

When shit gets real, our relationship stays intact.

I can be sure tomorrow, flying friends will be back.

To remind me I can fly too, even if my soul is black.

They seem to help me when I veer off-track

My army of darkness from above has my back.

Self-Love

I spent such a long time doing everything for those I love.

When I finally burnt out, I took it pretty rough.

I always gave it everything I had, evidently not enough.

When I fell, no one was offering a hand from above.

Self-love has proven one of my life's greatest challenges.

I nearly put myself in a hole with the abuse and damages.

No one left in my life apart from thieves and scavengers.

I had to drag my arse to my feet and tell him this.

"Just because nobody has been able to love you doesn't mean you should stop trying.

How many times must you return to this place? You are ill and dying.

Have you not had enough of sobbing and crying?

Love begins with you; anyone who says otherwise is lying."

Cursed

I've been suicidal my whole life but could never do the deed.

A suicidal impediment, my ending, I impede.

I was supposed to die young; everyone agreed.

Everyone is dying around me as I watch and bleed.

They all fear the reaper, whereas I goad it.

Take potshots at the sky, release the clip, and reload it.

To watch everyone die is my prize for the moment.

It's like a curse of invincibility, seeing others eroded.

Prey

I know I'm a fuckhead, and no one likes me.
It's a god sent cunts stopped trying to fight me.
Truth be told, I don't even like me.
But I'll stand my ground. Y'all can bite me.

An acquired taste you'll want to spit.
I find it really hard to give a shit.
Lacking taste? Lick my armpit.
Why would I care for the thoughts of a twit?

I'd be apprehensive if I were you, too.
I'm a comprehensive nut-certified lulu.
No harm, no foul, but I eat chickens too.
Too crazy in the coconut for you.

I'll do me, you do you, and we might be okay.
Be sure of your intentions before you come my way.
Games tend to get more serious the more you play.
I'm not keen on violence; it's in my veins.

Flare in the Skies

Sinking ships will drag you down.

If you stay too close, you're downward bound.

You die silently, drowning out the sound.

You completely disappear, unlikely to be found.

If you want to live, you'd best take note.

It's on you now to stay afloat.

Distance yourself from the ruined boat.

A sucker loves a sucker; it will have your throat.

Clinging to a sinking ship will ensure your demise.

There isn't any nobility in becoming its prize;

More like stupidity and arrogance epitomized.

Stay too close, and no one will hear your cries.

This theory is versatile and wise.

There will be many scenarios to which it applies.

Life is peculiar, but eventually, you realize:

Sinking ships are common murderers in disguise.

Eternally

Now, I've got my fear on the run.

Nowhere left to hide, nothing left undone.

Chasing my aversions down one by one,

Making love to the tension I'd once shun.

Always denied that I felt fear.

Now, fear feels me.

Always cried the dealt tear.

Now, fear has the mercy plea.

Those who dealt fear thought they had won.

They had no idea what they had done.

The catalyst of cruelty and abandon,

Left them riddled with nowhere to run.

Imposing, intimidating, taking control of me.

My choices made all that temporary.

Decomposing, deflating, you never had control of thee.

You only clutch fear eternally.

Oblivion

Have you ever been so lost you don't know who you are?

When you can't remember your name or the color of your car,

The evening becomes magical, as though you've never seen a star.

You have absolutely no clue how you arrived thus far.

You find yourself anxious yet simultaneously relaxed.

Being lost loses meaning when it's impossible to backtrack.

Time and space are an illusion that fails to make you perplexed.

Like Dora the explorer with no map in her backpack.

I'd always felt like a loser, but I'd never been that lost.

It was my mind I lost, and reality, the cost.

Tied in knots, unaware of the life I'd tossed.

No boxes left to tick everything had been crossed.

My biggest fear is going back to that place.

No control, no care, just a man without a face.

Haunted by what I was forced to erase.

I broke my son's heart and brought tears to his face.

Green Tomatoes

Don't feel fear just ask your husband.
I didn't mean to lift you; it got out of hand.
My girl and my mother each in one hand,
As I dropped any safe place to land.

I went to the brewery to celebrate,
I came home to a familiar land of hate.
In an effort to escape, I drank my beer in weight.
I stumbled, drunken, fell on my feet; I'd skate.

The helplessness your mother with cancer could only equate.
The pain you'd share with me was somewhat innate.
You left me in a dangerously volatile state.
You're damn lucky I didn't end you, mate.

The only dad I've ever known despised me with pure hate.
Father and mother parted the leftovers on my plate.
I knew nothing of it; my life he'd desecrate.
I vomited tomatoes as it spilled from my plate.

Shits and Giggles

I'm still reserved when it comes to tattoos and bikes.

I had a colourful childhood; all I can say is, yikes.

Traditionally, ink was for prostitutes and cons with stripes.

If you saw them on facebook, they'd be the ones with no likes.

I have prejudice, but I love art and the Harley Davidson.

However, it still conjures conflict for this wayward son.

The way it used to be, what they did done.

Makes me ashamed to buy a bike just for fun.

I don't need no tough stickers to intimidate some.

Don't need a bike so loud it busts your drum.

Don't need to associate with those who choose to be scum.

Clean skin and bikeless after the referendum.

I feel a betrayal of self has inevitably come.

To deny the things I love is invariably dumb,

Perhaps I should grow some balls and drink the rum. Illustrate
myself and buy that Harley Davidson.

Borne of Vibration

I've done my tour of duty on the front line.

In a place we see far more rain than sunshine,

You don't have to be in prison to be doing time.

I only survived because of the cunning stunts of mine.

Not a traditional warzone; times have changed.

We no longer fight with guns and bombs in range.

The entire control structure has been rearranged.

People are more blind than ever, and they don't think it strange.

It's a psychological war using emotional manipulation.

Everyone is involved in our human degradation.

A battle designed for millennia, with careful orchestration.

We are all just strings in the band, borne of vibration.

Would

I never want to be viewed with pity, only ever understanding.

I've been through a lot of shit, but I'm still standing.

I'm trying to leave the past back there and be outstanding.

To make the best of what's left is my future planning.

I don't know what's coming, but I know it will be better than the past.

It couldn't possibly have held on so long if I didn't allow it to last.

I've laid it to rest now; it's finally dead and passed.

I tried to kill myself, but it was not a blast.

I've fought my battles and conquered the demons I could.

Some will always remain tucked beneath my hood.

I'm better than I was, and to me, that's better than good.

I want to be met with love and compassion just as I would.

Healthy Wealthy and Wise

Today, on the menu is tuna and beans.

The sweet, sweet taste of poverty.

It's not that it's a hunger strike for me.

I just can't sell myself out for money.

Ramen noodles and salty baked potatoes.

What I wouldn't give for a fucking steak, though.

Shit food comes back up like a yo-yo.

There are many reasons I'm destined to roll solo.

It's not that I enjoy it by any means.

I just can't contribute to the world falling apart at the seams.

Most are more interested in jokes and memes.

Failing to realize they, too, are funny and obscene.

The paradise of the rich can only come from the hell of the poor.

People say it's a necessary evil, but I know the score.

If your evil is necessitated by needing more,

The only way to do that is fleecing from the poor.·

When

I'm sitting on my black album in an orange bag;

Like I rolled the meanest blunt, and I'm scared to take a drag.

I proved I ain't scared to wave my fuckin flag.

If you want it, come fuck with the big stag.

I'm not trying to be big; I'm not trying to be tough.

The world done what it done, and I've had enough.

I've trained for 38 years, the only way I know is rough.

Come to my front door if you are brave enough to call my bluff.

I'm a wolf; it's what I do. I huff n puff;

I won't hesitate to fuck you up and show you my stuff.

If the line gets crossed and you get a bit too gruff.

I'll teach a motherfucker when enough is enough.

Settling

I want to live, but I don't know how.

I've always chased death up until now.

That dream is dead; death won't allow.

He removed his hood and simply said ciao.

Now I'm stuck, sentenced to eternity, not just life.

I had no choice but to make the universe my wife.

We are betrothed now, for better or for strife.

I'm so sick of being on the pointy end of the knife.

I can't go back, but I'm struggling to make progress.

I committed to an oath, painted a picture of a bloody mess.

I'm trying to relax; this shouldn't be a source of stress.

It seems I'm trying to have it all by settling for less.

Mind Time

I'd like to stay in the recovery position until I can die.

I'd like to say this life has been lovely, but that would be a lie.

When I admit this, it's accompanied by a somber sigh.

I still don't understand, but I no longer question why?

The human condition is beyond a peculiar design.

Under the assumption, its complexities are greater than I.

I always refused to surrender, but now I must resign.

The mind is my enemy, and I must silence its cry.

I'm not a series of memories or imagination; I am now.

I am responsible for what I do and how.

Not yesterday and certainly not tomorrow, but right now,

The show is not over, but I feel like taking a bow.

It seems so impossible to clearly define

"The power of now" from Mr. Tolle helped me to find.

An escape from the torture of mind and time.

Life is pure hell in fast-forward or rewind.

Faceless

I forgot who I was for so long I don't want to be that anymore.

More than humbled by life, knees bruised from the floor.

I no longer know who I am or what's in store.

I just want to make the world richer in the areas so poor.

To serve a bigger purpose is my destiny. I'm sure. Being faceless and obsolete will assist to find the door.

Too long, I was self-obsessed, my focus internal war.

If I continue doing nothing, what is my life for?

My personal struggles are a reflection of a world plagued by woes.

"you don't know what you have til it's gone," so the saying goes.

I have a chance to make a difference; the pressure on me grows.

You can be part of the problem or part of the solution; everybody knows.

Divide and conquer is how we are defeated.

This is felt within me; from myself, I retreated.

No longer at war with myself but somewhat depleted.

Unite and rebuild is perhaps what is needed.

Unaddressed

Don't read it if you can't handle the pain.

A small glimpse of the hurt I feel every single day.

Some will laugh, some will cry, and some will be left in dismay.

My stories aren't pretty, but the flowers need the rain.

It all makes very little sense, but still, I try my best.

To salvage what I can and try to keep the rest.

My perception of self-image is what keeps me depressed.

So many things unsaid, so many issues unaddressed.

I'm still working on a better ending than the beginning.

I'm still physically ill, but the tables are turning.

For someone like me, life offers a slim chance of winning.

But I'll keep trying my absolute best as I continue learning.

As Such

My talent is really wasted here.

I've been stuck mainly due to fear.

Now I've got the wheel so I can steer,

trying to get my meat vehicle into gear.

I always hid myself; I mistook fear for humility.

I was terribly afraid to become all I can be,

I never resonated with the word impossibility,

But I caged myself and perpetuated hostility.

I've been like a dog who got beat too much.

I hid for safety, and pain was my crutch.

I became so lonely, desperate for a woman's touch.

It was meant to be that way; it was written as such.

I'm partially responsible for writing the story.

I only partly chose this category.

I do it for my children before I do it for me. My sacrifices are always for their glory.

Mutual Understanding

I speak many languages, all in the same tongue.

At a moment's notice, my mood had swung.

My mouth became vulgar like a song formerly sung.

So the message made it to the human acting like dung.

It's a crude delivery to get the message across

In my haste, I probably went too far, the point was not lost.

I felt he must understand the line he had crossed.

And hit the road like a rolling stone gathering no moss.

He parted with what seemed like a mutual understanding.

I huffed and puffed and blew the fire out, flames. I wasn't fanning.

I call him out for being a dick and the dumb shit he was planning.

I might just be his new idol because I'm fucking outstanding.

Art v Science

I try not to be too smart in the pursuit of art.

I sometimes shit myself just trying to fart.

Facts are poor expression, too far from the heart;

Reality and imagination are together but apart.

To provoke the senses and capture the mind,

Is what eyes are to someone who is blind.

Imagination can be dangerous; you will find.

Art should stimulate and not be confined.

Art is more than just observation and words.

It can rattle the comfortable or comfort the disturbed.

Painting creative pictures where facts can be curbed.

An artistic escape from reality is simply superb.

It can incite uncontrollable laughter or fits of rage.

It can cause vivid pictures to leap from the page.

A real fictional experience if I can set the stage.

Or share a piece of my heart with only ink on a page.

Mental Prison

I've been very disciplined in regards to remaining contained in my cage.

Paranoia, delusions, and mental illness have me frightened of the stage.

Managing myself is difficult, but the full moon helps me gauge

when I must imprison myself from fear of my impending rage.

I've never been well, a fact I can't deny.

I'm sure few have shook their fist more at the sky.

Will this joke make sense before I die?

Peculiar is funny; I'd like to laugh instead of cry.

Self-control: not so challenging for any other man.

How can this design flaw be a part of god's plan? I've heard of fight or flight, but I never ran.

I'm in the fight of my life, flying with a severed hand.

Heartbreak, misery, and trauma roll from my soul to stain the page.

Always needed something beyond therapy and burning sage.

I insist no one tampers with the lock on my little cage.

Unless one adequately prepares for the horror of my returning rage.

Calling

I don't know exactly when, where, or how,
I'm here for a purpose; my time is now
I feel it in my bones; my dreams I allow.
The field of dreams remains barren with no plough.

The power of belief is an amazing thing.
It can make a kind man kill or a pauper king.
We die without bees, and they're dying to sting.
Belief in myself is a prayer on a wing.

An overactive mind, a soft heart, and thick skin
Allowed me to believe that I just couldn't win.
Often my own worst enemy, living in sin,
Knowing I have a job to do with no place to begin.

Sense of duty so strong like a curse.
Too much sense like an overfull purse.
Not lacking, on the contrary, the reverse.
Desperately trying to locate it before the hearse.

At What Cost

Those struggling harder would be a slim minority.

Nevertheless, they have become a priority.

Victimizing themselves indirectly at the hands of authority.

Forced to live a life of pain, sadness, and poverty.

They say capitalism, but I see exploitation.

They say social structure, but I see orchestrated deception.

They say if you work harder in this competition.

You can have anything you want; it's your decision.

In order for one to indulge in luxury, it's invariably suffering for another.

The lifestyle we "earn" and the eyes and ears we cover.

Apparently, greed makes you more worthy than your brother.

Relentlessly scrambling to the top, treading on one another.

To attain what you have, what is the price you paid?

Without money, you can't even eat or get laid.

Starving and lonely, I'm beyond dismayed.

Rather than cut down the tree, I shall sit in the shade.

Reflectivity

Love is a concept more often misunderstood than comprehended.

In spite of this, we find ourselves confused that it ended.

When we feel like we're in love, there's nothing more splendid.

When we are destroyed by love, we feel we can't be mended.

We focus solely on the object of our affection.

Seldom aware our feelings are a reflection.

We do our best to establish a safe place void of inspection.

We fear we are unlovable; we're terrified of rejection.

We settle for someone who will spare us that torment.

We convince ourselves we are loved and content.

I thought I was in love a few times, but they all went.

Once they got what they wanted and, I was spent.

It was not them but my choice that made me see.

Love is a misunderstood game of reflectivity.

It seems to have lost its broad versatility.

When I need someone to mirror my heart back to me.

Tourniquet

I had a dream about people I once loved, now doing worse than me.

I couldn't relate more; our paths dictated by adversity.

I dreamt that they had learnt to treat themselves lovingly.

It provoked in me a competitive egocentricity.

I'd always struggled to be a friend to me.

I gravitated to broken souls unknowingly.

An unhealed child is a shameful identity.

I point the finger, but I too, am guilty.

In my dream, they both looked happy and healed.

I was not shocked at what this revealed.

I became defensive regarding my ego concealed.

I gauged myself against them; they were a shield.

Although it was only a dream, I hope they are moving in the right direction.

They've helped remind me the impossibility of perfection.

Since their betrayal, I took a vastly different direction.

When you remove the tourniquet to feel the love injection.

Then Some

I've lost at love more times than I care to mention.
Desperately seeking asylum, a refugee finds detention.
I try to hold back the tears; I guess it's residual retention.
I had to retreat from love and give up on life and then some.

Not exactly by choice, nor was it solely cause and effect.
I found my wits end, and my nervous system wrecked.
The shaking wouldn't cease, drowning in my own sweat.
Suicide was the only lonely word in my dialect.

I thought I had experienced love in my life.
I thought I found the one to be my wife.
My attempts at love went far beyond strife.
First her, then me, who tried to take my life.

Bad Company

Me, myself and Irene always see eye to I.

Complimentary and serene alone, I don't cry.

I was terrified of loneliness, but that well is dry.

I'm still afraid of me, but I'm a good guy.

Several relationships went awry.

They weren't selling what I needed to buy.

My fear of loneliness was created inside.

Forced countless times to wipe the tears I'd cry.

Being lonely and being alone are not the same.

I gave my heart to others; it was a crying shame.

When I picked up the pieces time and time again,

I taught myself to be alone, not lonely in pain.

Almost convinced I'm just a loser in this game.

I was bad company alone, so I attracted the lame.

I had my heart broken simple and plain.

Now I'm drunk and lost, cursing naked in the rain.

The Gift of Life

Becoming a father was the greatest experience I ever had.

I had no idea how to do it, but always wanted to be a dad.

The gift of a child was the pure love I'd never had;

My most monumental transition to good from bad.

The life I'd lead before my baby didn't make me proud.

The moment I laid eyes on him, I was floating on a cloud.

Instantly, a changed man desperate to figure out.

What love, protection, and guidance were all about.

I knew what not to do and figured I could guess the rest.

I promised myself and my boy to always try my best.

I'd never felt like a man before, and I'd never felt blessed.

The best day of my life, I felt my heart beating outside of my chest.

Absolutely consumed by love and a sense of duty to perform.

My outlook on life was vastly different the moment he was born.

A magical moment of instantaneous reform;

I vowed to heal my pain lest he feel the scorn.

Behind Enemy Lines

I got the PTSD, and people be testing me.

Setting off the fight or flight response repeatedly,

I don't like violence or what it brings out in me

Cause I never learned how to fly or just be.

I've learned to control it, but there is a boundary.

When the lines are crossed, and you behave disrespectfully.

As far as I'm concerned, if you violate my civil liberty.

I'm coming at you full force with absolutely no mercy.

Liberty doesn't need defining, but for you to embody it and see.

That liberation is freedom for those who choose to be free.

I try to rid myself of lingering anger very promptly.

Anger is nothing more than a guide; never something to be.

Poor Boy

I was left to raise my baby alone when his mother bailed to be a whore.

That disgusting creature literally spat in my face as she walked out the door.

I did my best to raise my son, the boy I love and adore.

For her, it must have been too much like a chore.

I bent over backward to keep her in his life, I couldn't have done more.

I vacated my own home fortnightly so my son wouldn't be sore.

After a year of sacrifices, I said, "You can't stay here anymore."

For the next two years, she disappeared, leaving our son's wound raw.

I don't know where she went or what she did it for.

But she decided to re-emerge not long after he turned four.

She thought she had grounds to come at me with the law.

She typically lied under oath, so many lies she swore.

Once again, that bitch got shown the door.

She tried to take him from me, I guess to hurt me more.

After fourteen years, a suicide attempt had me unconscious on the floor.

He spent six months with his mother and asked me, "Why are you so poor?"

Guardian Angel

My son hates it when I swear, so I try to refrain from using foul words in my art.

I say try because sometimes my wholehearted expression is to say, "You're a shit cunt," straight from the heart.

He doesn't understand my struggles and issues, and from that, I kept him apart.

So when he hears me swear, he quickly reminds me I'm polluting his senses like a fart.

He'll never understand the damage I'm trying to overcome.

I try to respect his wishes and avoid using fuck and cunt.

There's nothing I wouldn't do for my beautiful, caring son.

Most times, I can drop the slugs from my loaded gun.

I'm proud that my boy despises those words.

I'm ashamed that he heard them in my voice first.

I try so hard to be better than my dads were,

Words are only words that exposure is far from the worst.

He's helping me heal, pointing to where residual pain lies.

It's so hard to see in the absence of love, looking through strained eyes.

He's my guardian angel who brought love to my life.

He doesn't need to hear language distasteful or rife.

Treasure Box

Some gold coins and pearls in here, but the treasure is all mine.

Pirate Pauly, the poet of words, done poorly.

If you don't get it, it can't be your fault, surely.

Piracy left me with scurvy, and I'm out of time.

I sailed the seven deadly seas and tasted the seven sins.

At this point, I'm no longer even hoping that heaven wins.

I'm far from evil, but sometimes temptation wins.

An old pirate I will die abandoned treasure box within.

I speak in riddles, metaphors, analogies, and cryptic enigma.

Often about the guilt, sores, misery, and stigma

Pirates aren't understood, let alone accepted.

Polly wants a cracker. He just shit down my peg leg.

Tangled Mess

I'm so tired, and still, I can't sleep.

So sad, yet still, I can't weep.

What I need is locked inside too deep.

Rolling with no brakes down a hill too steep.

Cleaning my mind is no easy mission.

Not quite as simple as making a decision.

It more closely resembles an exorcism.

Fighting an infinite source of power like nuclear fission.

They say there is a fine line between genius and madness.

The line got blurry, like the one between anger and sadness.

I'm such a mess; counting sheep is pointless.

I suppose I'll write through the night, untangling my stress.

Hard to Breathe

I'm really fucked up. I know this
It took so long to afford me my focus.
Offering what I needed to bad jokers,
I put it back in me and hocus pocus.

I neglected and abused myself to the point of suffocation.
I loathed myself and became my proprietor of mutilation,
Hurting the person I hated most till cumulation.
Destroyed myself from the inside out, no hesitation.

A freight train to nowhere, no stops, no station.
I couldn't kill myself directly, making a recreation.
Always wanted to die, having fun on the way home, found the
end of the line: internal strangulation.

Only shallow breaths, my right lung is restricted.
Dying on the inside, my emotions depicted:
Nicotine, THC, and amphetamines are listed.
I smoked so much goading the reaper, not cause I'm addicted.

When I struggle to breathe, no panic, heart is steady.
I'm not afraid to die; I've always been ready.
Sold myself out for an existence so empty.
Lung cancer will probably answer my death plea.

Wanker

I made peace with my maker, and I've never felt greater.

We were at war; I became a chronic masturbator.

An interesting protest, to say the least, ice in the incinerator.

It's nice to say bye to that shit, and I won't see you later.

I was a counter-intuitive, spiteful, and destructive creator.

I was the master of my own misery, my world's dictator.

I didn't want to face I, my fear; I would cater.

Always obsessed with my meat below the equator.

Societal manipulation had my balls in a vice.

Life was a struggle eating butter-flavoured rice.

Preservation took so much effort, it wasn't very nice,

I beat my meat cause they used my balls against me, my six-inch sacrifice.

Stunted

There is something queer about the people here.

Watching me intently, perhaps out of fear

They have a desperation to know dirt, not an idea.

Pity falls short, oh my dear.

It's curious, to say the least.

Why would anyone choose bones to feast?

A bit fucked up, like a child and a priest.

Where do they hide when their laughter has ceased?

Maybe it's the tears of a clown or the agony of a beast.

It's sad either way, attacking others in search of peace.

Sadness comes in many forms; happiness doesn't tease.

So disgusted by themselves, they need another for release.

I wouldn't wish it on anyone, not even my enemies;

A painful way to live, dying on your knees.

If I were offended, I'd be fooled by their desperate hidden pleas.

Misery cloaked in cruelty, these eyes can spot with ease.

Are they a bit slow or simply easy to deceive?

Why do they persist when their pain, they can't relieve?

Grown-ups that couldn't grow up is still so hard to believe.

Desperately clinging to their method with no hope of reprieve.

Tattoos

Tattoos I refuse, wearing my scarred art on my sleeve.

I spill my pain with ink to express and relieve.

Only ever understood by the way you perceive.

Like pictures on one's skin, perception can deceive

Like the making of a human, you must give a fuck to conceive.

I could paint my epidermis, but the flashbacks wouldn't leave,

Creating images with ink desperately seeking reprieve.

Art is subjective and personal, borne from what I believe.

Beliefs shaped from experiences I know I can never escape.

Broken on the inside using ink like glue or tape.

The images become clearer as my suit of ink takes shape.

As I spill sorrow with ink, my open wounds still gape.

It's all I can do for healing. I don't expect you to understand.

I spent far too long perpetuating my pain, my hand at my command.

Hurting myself repeatedly, compelled by the hurt of another man,

Sickened by the burden of another, alone, I take a stand.

Forsaken

I feel I've been waiting forever for my forever sleep.

Death evades me daily; that hooded clever creep.

It too often feels like a harvest I shall never reap.

I wish I'd experienced more "mountain-high" and less "river-deep."

It saddens me to realize what I view as life's prize.

Not even a cliche about finish lines and nice guys.

Life wears a mask, for everyone, a different disguise.

For many, as they part, there will be no sad goodbyes.

Whether it's all by design or chaos in the making,

I was forced to resign that my life's not worth taking.

As I slowly re-align amidst the pain and aching.

I couldn't kill myself this life I'm still forsaking.

Sorrow Borrow

I spent so long on bad habits I'm lost without them.
I don't know the man in the mirror, a half-dead specimen.
Riddled with shame and pain whilst coughing phlegm.
The thorn in my side, my rose's stem.

A gift from me with a chaser of regret,
A slow, painful death approaches and the stage is set.
It was never permanent; this life is to let.
I wrecked the rental. I deserve what I get.

Suicidal from the start, I never wanted this life.
Self-loathing, self-destructive proprietor of strife.
I understand and care more with the joy of hindsight.
Eventually, one must fall, living on the edge of a knife.

When it was only me, I wanted death; life, I couldn't bear
Now, the best part of me is my son, the love we share.
Soon, I'll be only a memory, and he'll become aware.
Choices I made took me too soon; his heart will tear.

His memory of me will be tainted with resent.
It's justified I left it too late to repent.
It will kill him too soon when I'm hell sent.
He'll understand my final gift to him was agony lent.

Molecular Dance

I find it inspiring that atoms and molecules are behind this molecular dance.

I'm no scientist, but I know it didn't happen by chance.

To ponder and observe it puts me in a dream-like trance,

All the magic of creation at a single glance

Not only inspired, I feel somewhat connected.

Not too indifferent nor rejected.

When this dawned on me, the feeling was splendid

I don't need science to appreciate it; it doesn't need to be dissected.

I just marvel in appreciation and amazement.

As I'm a part of it functioning adjacent,

Sometimes I wonder where my brain went.

It was fixated on a dandelion growing through the pavement.

Offerings

I seem to be growing positive as the world grows colder.

Perception is malleable in the eyes of the beholder.

As I step more comfortably into my skin, I'm a little bolder.

This world will be a better place when I'm done, just like I told her.

I've released many burdens that gripped me incessantly.

I have developed better habits and personal strategies.

I no longer play the blame game; woe is not me.

I simply want to find happiness by offering gifts sincerely.

I've always loved language and literature of all sorts.

Writing has always helped me assess and clarify my thoughts.

Poetry helped me rid ills that made my body contort.

This amazing outlet exposed the me I always sought.

It's like a two-way street, the more I give, the more I receive.

I'm shocked at the crippling ailments; it's relieved.

I'm far more intuitive, in myself I can believe

Whereas prior to poetry, I was prone to hide and deceive.

Alone in Reserve

I'm happy to wait patiently for what I deserve.

I don't expect the moon or a star; I don't expect the earth.

I won't settle for anything less than a lover who appreciates my worth.

Until the day I feel that I'm content to stay alone in reserve.

Love has not treated **me! kindly,** myself I did not preserve.

I dived in whole-heartedly never putting my needs first.

Relationships went from bad to worse, then worse to worst.

Like driving full speed at a head-on collision, no attempt to swerve.

I was completely blind; my relationship with me needed work.

I worked so hard to no avail, as she used me with a smirk.

I was invested, loyal and faithful, smitten with my jerk.

She chipped away and made me weak, the work I didn't shirk.

I have come a long way since that day, many things I've learned.

Some lessons impossible to forget, still scarred from being burned.

If only I'd known myself better, perhaps I would have turned.

When it comes to love and companionship, respect must be earned.

Taking Shots

I carry guilt so heavy that my knees shake and buckle.

Suffocated by shame, to avoid tears, I fake a chuckle.

I live by the sword and probably die by tooth and knuckle.

Naked and alone on the reaper's teat, I suckle.

I can't blame death for the hell I live.

I own every choice; it's myself, I can't forgive.

The lesser of two evils always left me less to give.

I torture myself with the parts I'd kill to re-live.

Life has been far from kind in many ways.

I've convinced myself so many times there will be better days.

All I know ,I had to learn the hard ways.

The test offers the lesson, and I'm the one who pays

I try to be mindful and let go of the past.

Always put on the spot; learning comes last,

I think, with my brain but live from my heart.

Only one shot at life; a high calibre blast.

Two Words

Do things your morrow self will thank you for.

It's you that makes living such a chore.

The work your yester self left at your door.

Will be the tomorrow, the next day and forevermore.

It's not that hard to scrub the dishes and wash the floor.

Until depression grips you firmly in its claw.

All of a sudden, you weigh one hundred kilos more.

Apathy and despair are winning the war.

Every cell of your body is flooded like before.

Your ten-ton skeleton is weary and sore.

Tomorrow will be harder; anxiety will ensure.

You want to get up, but two words taunt you "WHAT FOR?"

You feel weak, sick, and paranoid, for sure.

Spent decades navigating this design flaw.

It's affected every aspect of life, ashamed to the core.

The day you die, you won't have to fight anymore.

Charlie Bucket List

It all just is

I finally surrendered to the abyss.

So dramatic, like bubbles and fizz.

My brain was absent for the pop quiz.

The night before Christmas, so it is,

Expecting much of the same, the Charlie Bucket List.

Rarely disappointed, I get the gist.

Cut from a different cloth, hooked on the piss.

I finally learned the Wonka sweetness.

Whilst those I'd have died for had me settle for less,

Nasty children will learn in bitterness.

The price one must pay for success.

Basket Case

ADHD hates me.
It's the way they made me maybe.
The hardest thing for me to be
Is still, calm, and solitary.

I was a bull at a gate, always on the go.
The only speed I knew was not slow.
I did what felt natural; how was I to know?
As I was running, I was also hiding on the low.

Chasing my own tail, going nowhere fast,
I don't even have a tail: just an arse.
Anything to stay busy, from building houses to mowing grass.
I understand my compulsive tendencies at last.

To be alone, still, and calm has become my task.
To communicate with my body, to listen and ask.
Why would I hide behind such a tiresome mask?
Mental illness is a shameful place to bask.

Caged Hearts

I take ridicule, hatred, deceit, and loathing.
Then, return your child in new clothing.
The immense ill in my heart will not see me folding.
I'll fight the good fight without withholding.

The gifts you gave me I couldn't let go.
Even though it killed me to carry that burden alone.
Wanting nothing but death, memories cut to my bone.
Straight from your heart, the present I couldn't throw.

Pure expression of your bitter soul.
The residual burns like a fire I hold.
I guess we all choose which way we go.
When they made you, it was from a different mould.

You sold yourself out to behave so low.
The person that broke you wasn't me, no.
Your work here is done; enjoy the show.
The first tear was mine, but the last is to go.

When you leave the show, you will undoubtedly know.
The taste of bitter tears for the seeds you sew,
Your pain is worse. Want to know how I know?
Because you can't stop an avalanche with an echo.

You surrendered to your enemy and sold your soul.
No good deed goes unpunished; rewards you will hold.
Your worthy companion whom with which you'll grow old.
Your shadow will bother you, and your reflection will scold.

Now I feel like Milhouse with too many souls
as you row in circles in your boat with holes.
You made a mockery of my love as you achieved your goal.
You can't have mine, and you will never feel whole.

For someone so weak, it was mighty bold.
To assume you could wreck my heart and steal my soul,
I weathered the storm and kept my heart gold
You became your abuser, and that shit is old.

I said what I said

You ain't gonna come across poetry this deep, this raw, this fucking Wow.

You can just go ahead and show me the money right now.

Take it to the printing press, or however they do it, not sure how.

But share my stories and ideas so I can make a difference somehow.

It's not even about money, though I could use a cash cow.

It's a burning in my soul that just won't back down.

I'm jumping in for a bomb dive; gonna make a splash now.

I'll find a way to make a difference; I don't give a fuck how.

The wetter, the better, was how I always said it.

Rather it be something I said than regret it.

Bitches get wet when I make a splash; you can bet it.

If I said it, I meant it; I didn't say you will get it.

Maybe a musician could turn it into song.

Reach the Chest like the medicine bong.

It feels so right; I'll take the gamble I'm wrong.

Instead of crushing my dreams, I invite you to dream along.

Vacation

I've been experiencing wave after wave of inner tranquility.

Conscious desire coupled with factors occurring unexplainably.

It came about both deliberately and through destiny.

I've never been so at peace, surrendered to serenity.

A sort of transcendental meditation.

A removal of my mental location.

I opened a vault with some hesitation.

Much more relaxing than any vacation.

Ironically, vacation was vital to the process,

out with the old made way for progress.

It happened so fast, almost simultaneous.

I'm coming up short, trying to explain this.

Every hair on my body became erect,

Better than any drug you could inject.

I was heavy yet floating. I can recollect.

Like something inside works when I thought it was wrecked.

Chuckles Next Door

People mock me and joke with loud laughter.

I like being the bud of a joke; flowers bloom thereafter.

I stay in my own lane, ignorant like a pastor.

It's not my business, but the voice of happiness is laughter.

If cruelty, ignorance, and judgment serve them so well.

I don't take it as personally, as their living hell.

I follow their lead and utilize ignorance as well.

Happiness has clearly run dry in their wishing well.

It's a horrible coping mechanism I've seen before.

They needed a way out and made me their door.

If putting shit on me makes them a little less sore,

I hope they piss themselves rolling on the floor.

Getting nasty or upset won't settle a score.

Even if the joke is bad or their taste is poor.

They should laugh so hard they cramp in the jaw.

Laughter is the voice of happiness, we could all use some more.

The Order of Love

Love and I have never quite seen eye to eye.

As illusions of love dissipate me and my hatred cry.

Raised with abandonment and neglect, I've never been able to rise.

Never learning to love myself made loneliness my prize.

I've been preyed upon by women using love as their guise.

Fooled over and over turned my foolishness to despise.

My desperation for love; a magnet for deception and lies.

Used for everything I had and everything I was, I'm left with no disguise.

The less I have, the less I get. Nobody even tries.

Stripped naked with all dignity taken; how the time flies.

They took everything and left me empty, just a little more wise.

My failure to understand love, inside naivety, and hope dies.

When you have nothing left to offer, only disparity and sighs.

They don't even pretend to love you; that's what ignorance buys.

Love has a very strict order; with only me, it can initialize.

It's not easy to love the man they exploited when all he does is cries.

Eleven

Life is such a multi-faceted, multidimensional mind fuck.

Senses, colours, frequencies, and waves this whole thing has me awe-struck.

Such a wondrous spectacle, and I've been missing it in my mind, stuck.

I don't know how to respond to it all. I probably need some dumb luck.

Sometimes, I don't know if the world is ill or my mind is full of muck.

There seems so much wrong with what I see, but no one gives a fuck.

I suspect it's an involuntary partnership, like a trailer and truck.

Moving along in the wrong direction, trailing along stuck.

I want to improve the world but don't know where to begin.

Why is it not obvious? Why must I point out evil and sin?

Everyone is competing in a race I don't want to win.

I want to trip everyone and kick them in the shin.

Without people, life on earth would be heaven.

In terms of deadly sins, I'm sure there are more than seven.

If there is a hell, nearly all will be sent then.

That one and this one will resemble eleven.

Dad

My child's love makes my life worth living.

Not much else in a world so unforgiving.

The reason I continue trying and striving.

My child is my world, but what world am I giving?

When I am gone, he is the legacy.

I don't just make my bed; I make his, you see.

When I lie straight, he gets wrinkled sheets.

When I forsake Mother Nature, his bed is soiled with pee.

Cause and effect: collaborate as a team.

The cause I choose, the effect he'll redeem.

Just as the fabric is stitched and connected by a seam.

Generations inevitably adhere to this theme.

He offers me purpose and responsibility.

He truly loves me just for being me.

For that reason, I do my best to lead. Before I make his bed, I wash the sheets.

Indifference

I want to improve this shit show and make the world a better place.

Direction is more important than speed; some things I can't erase.

The journey I choose begins with a mirror in the face.

Going nowhere fast, I already won that race.

I don't know how to do it, but the key is understanding.

Having a key with no door makes it impossible for planning

Blind hope is all I have, but as long as I'm still standing.

I seek a better life for our children, no evil reign commanding.

The more I observe and understand, the more I despise the human race.

Just like me going nowhere fast, running in place.

To identify as human the catalyst of my disgrace.

Tell your kids they don't deserve better, and be sure to look them in the face.

It may be bold and unreasonable to believe I can make a difference.

I know one man can do it, and Jesus Christ is my reference.

I can't ignore it or participate in complacence.

If I can make life better for my child, it will have made sense.

Doubt

People are so quick to label and judge as if they know who I am.

These little poems offer clues to understand.

Self-expression is therapeutic but on the other hand.

I highly doubt I'll be understood in conditioned minds so bland.

Those who are "better than me" and insist on competition

will never be able to grasp my life's mission.

It's a disturbing reality of the human condition.

I have no desire to get those people to listen.

It may seem paradoxical or hypocritical to many;

who am I to make a judgement on any?

Even if they see me sociopathic, obsessed with plenty.

If money blows your hair back, I'll bet you a twenty.

My doubt is as valid as your self-appointed superiority.

We are from two very different worlds, seemingly.

Perhaps my need to be understood is the source of inferiority.

It seems the larger one's ego, the less room they have for
empathy.

Starving Artist

I'm pretty sure I qualify as a starving artist.

I eat pretty well, but I'm starved of life's goodness.

Compassion, purpose, love, or a woman's touch,

All these things have a price tag attached.

I don't think it is food the artist longs for,

Nor money or applause the singer writes songs for.

It's not immortality for the sculptor.

I think they're all love-scorned, mistreated, and sore.

It may very well have been days since I've eaten.

Food seems unimportant when your heart and soul are beaten.

How do I replace what was taken by the cretins?

Without being forced to commit similar sins?

Describe it in my art's description.

Paint a vivid, detailed depiction.

Rely upon art like my addiction.

A starving artist with the artist's affliction.

Monkey Business

I'm giving serious consideration to becoming a monk.
Celibacy and sobriety are too easy for this punk.
I'll do just about anything to get out of this funk.
When I'm really honest with myself, my life has always stunk.

Enlightenment sounds delightful because I feel so heavy.
My mind, heart, and spirit all are weary.
Like a heavy downpour promising to break the levee,
When I think back or look forward, my eyes become teary.

The life I've lead has worn me down.
Show me the crucifix in a thorny crown,
Stone me to death in the middle of town,
Or shave my head and hand me a gown.

Their ideas, beliefs, and customs somewhat align with mine.
I don't really want to live lavishly and wine and dine.
I could just chop wood, carry water, and wait for my sign.
I could just keep it very simple until I walk the line.

Willow Dance

My willow dances in the wind.

Means my previous words, I rescind.

As my judgements and thoughts have thinned,

What's important is on my mind.

I claimed to be an oak; I refused to sway or bend.

I became a sad joke; I preferred to play instead of mend.

Always racing the clock, from tomorrow, I would lend.

In all ways disgracing, I'd mock; I borrowed all I was able to send.

I thought I had to stand unwavering in what I believed to be true.

My life was bland, unsavory for what I perceived and misconstrue.

This belief or ideal, like an oak tree inside me, the seed grew.

The self-destructive capacity of beliefs, I didn't have a clue.

Now, I feel like a willow dancing in a haze of blue.

Still strong, confident, and unwavering but flexible, too.

To encompass all of nature is something you'll be amazed to do.

To experience God should be felt by all, not restricted to a few.

I Know

It tickles your brain a lot more to go with the flow.

I used to be the type to put on a show.

Emotionally retarded, in some areas, a bit slow.

At least, that's what I thought, but now I know.

I created the hell inside. I had no choice but to grow.

The hardest thing I ever did was completely let go.

Every belief, every thought, every seed I sow.

That was the reason I nearly resorted to blow.

It would have been the end of me and put me below.

I was suicidal and ill, my soul black as a crow.

I pulled my head out of my arse and let my slow arse grow.

I committed to myself and surrendered to I AM, and now I know.

Final Say

The demons be knowing when the poems keep flowing.

There is something underlying preventing my growing.

The ultimate rebellion is awareness and knowing.

But I'm just not knowing what's stopping my growing.

There must be something still there, lingering resent.

I just can't put my finger on why I'm not content.

My life has been a stinger; I can only represent.

I thought I'd purged it all, but some demons are still pent.

I will release the evil I've absorbed if it's the last thing I do.

My soul will be light, and your sins will be on you.

I didn't deserve the cruelty and punishment you put me through.
On your deathbed, it's between my man and you.

Condemnation

My life was hell and largely my own making.

I knew of God but rejected love self-condemnation.

I trudged through the mud for decades, forsaking.

I wade my way through the flames until self-obliteration.

When I realized what I had done, I couldn't be complacent.

I was not myself; I blamed others and God for my placement.

Like another living my life as I watched adjacent.

I had to remove many demons and die inside before my replacement.

Only the core elements of who I was still remain,

The ones my enemies promised me would be slain.

It's like I was begging for it, saying, "Fill me pain."

My teacher used to call me a dill; this dill I will retrain.

Exemplary

I had to re-birth myself and then learn how to parent me.

I had to dispel my bad habits and do it coherently.

I never wanted to; I forced myself to do it for me

If I ever wanted to understand the love of all mighty.

It's been terrifying and liberating simultaneously;

I'm no longer sighing or waiting anxiously.

I have a path to take and the eyes to see

Nothing means more than for my son to see exemplary.

The sun gets brighter as it rises in the sky.

As I continue to rise, I feel it inside.

The relationship between all things, I cannot deny

I never felt such emotion, like that I never cried.

Zen n Now

Perception is malleable in the eyes of the beholder, and every devil has an advocate.

Preference does not dictate truth; lies get bolder, and evil doesn't wait.

Patience is a virtue I heard from someone older, and I thought they were fucking great.

But it was only the way I perceived it; they helped design my inevitable fate.

Consequences are a given; it's your conscience that determines the severity.

Looking forward to success, but only in hindsight can we find clarity.

If your success depends upon suffering and placing others in poverty

You have succeeded at selling your soul; nothing left of you worth a penny.

There is a special place in hell for those souls, so easy to sell.

They believe that life is swell as they make their fellow man unwell.

It's not my story to tell but fuck, I tell it well,

A man who represents himself has a fool for a client, but at least he can spell.

Inherent

I spent an awfully long time blaming my parents for things they did wrong.

I became a broken record repeating the same terrible song,

Stuck in a self-destructive loop for way too long.

I didn't realize they were doing their best with what they knew all along.

I was angry and spiteful, but deep down, I was really devastated.

I didn't know how to take it, so I did what was demonstrated

I began to see myself through their eyes, so myself, I hated.

When I realized I was way off the mark, I was humiliated.

I began to heal and change when I came to understand

They were growing and learning; in life, nothing goes as planned.

They could only do what they knew, with no one lending a hand.

Maturity can take a lifetime; over many years, it's spanned.

When I became a parent myself, I began to see things a bit different.

We all have issues with our parents, and then we become a parent.

In facing the issues ourselves, the paradigm becomes transparent.

We try our best, and sometimes, we mess up, and that is inherent.

Anomaly

They don't make it easy for me to want to do what I love.

I can't even please myself without programming, and shame is giving me a shove.

Should I feel bad for the way I was made by the lord above? I got needs not being met. Are we all just doing improv?

Is it just me or is it lacking clarity for all?

Occasionally, things are crystal clear, but that window is so small.

Square, circle, or triangle, I always seem to hit the wall.

In this game, I question who is to rise and who is to fall.

You cannot fathom the power; I'm something of an anomaly.

The gift I was endowed with will fuck you up properly.

I try not to be a dick as my appendage hangs floppily.

Why is life so hard when I'm the only one stopping me?

Good in the Hood

You start to tell lies, and it multiplies.

A veil of dishonesty to disguise your lies.

It becomes obsessive-compulsive to guys in the guise.

Women are not excluded. I've seen lies in their eyes.

To make a mockery of reality and hear your loved one's cries.

What is your entity but a perpetrator? How time flies.

Time is a mere measurement, the dash that is your life

With the time you were given, did you sell your soul or use it wise?

A soul is a funny thing and, more often than not, misunderstood.

It's not the life you lead, the body you know, or the brain beneath the hood.

It is the underlying essence, the knowledge, the wisdom to be good.

If God is good, it's all good in the hood; I may never be understood.

Elf

You've got all the things, but you haven't got yourself.

I'm not impressed by your ego or your wealth.

Missing the point out of ignorance, it's not stealth.

On your deathbed, you will realize you came up short, like an elf.

Distractions, sensory pleasures, and competition keep you blinded.

If you're not even looking for yourself, you will never find it

You'll say I worked so hard for all of this; I really grinded.

When your time nears its end, you'll wish you could rewind it.

Looking back at the false claims of your identity,

You'll probably feel even more foolish than me.

All the effort you wasted only to feel empty.

You must pass this level to get to the next, how it's meant to be.

Servant

Some days, I'm on fire, and other days I just burn

Sometimes, I feel I should retire, but I still have so much to learn.

I'm still allowing myself to rewire and not be too stern.

On a good day, my only desire is to sit in a garden beneath a fern.

I always put too much pressure on myself, often to my detriment.

To finally find my peace has been absolutely heaven-sent.

I'm still unsure of my purpose, searching for fulfillment.

I'm sure it will be found in helping others; I'm supposed to be a servant.

In exchange for heaven only found in the divine.

I devote my life to service; even when I'm bound with swine.

I'm getting fatter; I'm a little round but still fine.

I got my fill of goodness and still hit the ground with cheap wine.

Free

I feel like I'm freefalling in a bottomless pit.

I made the choice and decided to want less shit.

I eliminated the old me under duress with grit.

I still poke fun at the past with my impressive wit.

I'm no longer in limbo, feeling like the journey never ends,

always on the road navigating traffic and bends.

Finally moving in the right direction as my body and soul mends,

I'm comfortable free-falling thanks to some very clever friends.

As I plummet, I feel more grounded than ever before.

The only way was falling if I was to find the floor.

I was desperate for some things to be less and some to be more.

I'm at terminal velocity in the abyss, and I've never been more sure.

Recollection

Underlying it all, I want the best for everyone.

I'm not crying at all when this shit is said n done.

I was supposed to be dead already, to the best of my recollection.

They said I would be dead or in jail by 18 and then some.

I came out on top, and now they're all nervous and curious.

A one-stop shop to provide service and be furious

They gave me a lot of pain and promise; I had to stew on this.

I healed alone, and now I'm impervious and glorious.

An experience I'll never get again, so I'd best make the most of it.

Like the bomb in the letter, terroristic postal shit

You will get the message, and I won't have to boast or quit.

I just came here to inform you of what you're gon get.

Language Universal

The universe speaks to me
From a singing bird to a dying tree,
I never heard it before; you see
I didn't even know it was a problem for me.

A complex head full of complicated trickery.
My ignorance and ego danced merrily.
Too engrossed in the struggles within me.
The answer is so simple, hiding with irony.

To some, it comes so naturally.
They could always hear the hypnotic melody.
The power of the universe guiding them softly.
As they thrived and flourished, I yearned to be free.

Trying too hard to be the best possible me.
Turned me into a dog chasing its tail, proverbially
The universe didn't change its language or frequency.
It continued to speak even to me.

Falling on deaf ears frustratingly,
My good intentions were my enemy.
Me against the universe is futility,
The pressure on me, so too the responsibility.

I didn't trust the answer was somewhere externally.

Assumed it was just punishment for a mystery.

The price paid for ignorance was more than costly.

I literally lost everything and gained insanity.

Beyond broken, I cried on my knees.

"If you're up there cunt help me, please."

I shuddered with goosebumps in a sudden cold breeze.

In a moment, I lost all ego and vanity.

I felt like a blind man who could suddenly see.

All I ever need, the universe presents to me.

I had to die inside thoroughly.

Before I could hear the dialect and begin to read.

She needs no words for in that breeze.

She said, "Now you're ready. I know you feel me."

A language so vast, cloaked in secrecy

Provides the essentials for the mortal journey.

She continues with an heir of grand subtlety.

Whether willing or unwilling, I hope everyone grasps a language universally.

It may be just a pipe dream.

I distinctly heard her whisper, "It's a possibility."

"If you could learn this language, plant a seed.

You know very well the cost of ignoring me.

How many more must be brought to their knees?

Perhaps it's your turn to help me, please.

No one is immune, not even the bees,

so few can hear the words I speak.

I destroyed you to make you humble, not weak.

You are part of something whole, much like the trees*11*

I believed I was a failure perpetually.

Ignoring this communication complacently.

The day I heard the universe beckon me,

She said sweetly, "I'll do the rest; just plant the seed."

Pantomime

I still hurt myself all the bloody time.

Covered in scars, I try to reason and rhyme.

My life would scare the pants off you, crime after crime.

In an invisible box with no voice, I am a mime.

Dressed in black with a pale face, expressionless.

To express something through motion is quite a test.

In a box without a voice, I try my best.

Sending a message with movement to show the rest.

Imprisoned by history and dark thoughts, I confess

—my view of myself, life, and its stress.

I try to convert it to art to impress.

Still, I remain in a box you can't see voiceless.

The contrast of white gloves meets black sleeves.

Like Superman in a wheelchair, Mr Reeves.

The black clothes suggest what was done to me,

Whereas the white gloves indicate what I'm offering.

Bend over Backwards

All of my experiences Everything I've seen

All of my destinations Everywhere I've been

All of my soul Everything unseen

All of my limbo Everything between

All of my wants Everything I need

All of my destruction Everything I seed

All of my breath, Every drop I bleed,

All of my love Everyone I freed.

9 798889 795385 1